Dark ANGEL

AN UNEARTHLY SINS NOVEL

Stefanie Dawn

Dark Angel
An Unearthly Sins Novel

Stefanie Dawn

ISBN: 978-1763870444

Editing and Proofing by Swish Design & Editing
Book Design by Swish Design & Editing
Cover Design by Opium House Creatives
Published by Angels and Fire Books
Cover Image Copyright 2022

DEDICATION

To everyone who's more creative and funnier
at dedications than I am.

Dark Angel

AN UNEARTHLY SINS NOVEL

PROLOGUE

EMRICK

Ten Years Ago...

Turning back to face him, I was thankful for the rain that obscured his form, making his body a mere shape moving through the downpour. Because without the rain, my tears would be visible to my brother and not hidden by the streaking on my cheeks made up of polluted water from the clouds hanging above the smog. The night was perfect for my mood—when my world was falling apart the skies opened up and grieved with me. I'm sure he could see the tears anyway, but he knew better than to say anything about it. Zaqiel may be older than me, but it didn't mean I wasn't above kicking the shit out of him.

Crying.

Even the word sounded weak.

A human weakness I never thought I'd submit to. But it wasn't only due to sorrow—that emotion had been smothered beneath layers of sheer rage, and I intended to keep the pain there, hidden where it belonged. White-hot anger burned through my body and threatened to melt my skin. My wings were out, off-whites and pale grays against the dark of the night as Zaqiel and I stood in some dirty fucking alleyway having a pointless squabble about fate and right and wrong.

He didn't know right from wrong, not in this world. Zaqiel hadn't yet spent much time out of the Silver City and still believed humanity was as good and faithful to Father as we were.

As I *was.*

"Come home, Emrick," he said.

That fucking soothing voice of his only pushed daggers further into my soul. Because it was all fake, even if he thought it was real. It was simply default for Zaqiel to attempt to calm every situation, to be the voice of reason—the angel to soothe the angels. The entire system was shot to hell, including his pacifying voice and the sympathy he portrayed.

Zaqiel was only pretending to understand my anger, but he couldn't, not really, and I'd have preferred if he had outright said he didn't understand but respected my decision with how I planned to deal with it. But all I was met with was pitying looks and lectures on the *right* thing, the *good* thing, like it's always so simple.

He had a lot to learn.

"Forget the troubles of Earth," he said. "Come home."

Shaking my head, the droplets of water ran from my dark hair, flicking off and disappearing into the haze of the rain as it intensified. Barreling down on the dumpsters around us, I had to raise my voice to be heard over the downpour as though God was trying to drown me out with nature.

He'd never control me again.

"I'm going to kill those men, Zaqiel, and you can't stop me."

His expression was stony, it always was. Zaqiel— always in control, the level-headed brother, the older, the wiser. "You know the rules."

"Fuck the rules," I cried, throwing my hands up. He flinched, and I relished in his momentary loss of stoic control. "Demons kill humans all the fucking time."

"Not always. That's not true, and you know it."

"But sometimes." I stepped forward, my boots splashing in the puddles on the ground, announcing my approach, although he didn't flinch or move away. Then we were nose to nose, same height and build, his blue eyes not wavering from my deep brown, so dark they were almost black. "*Sometimes,* Zaqiel, and isn't *sometimes* already too many? Why are demons allowed to get away with murder, but I cannot?"

"They don't get away with murder, brother. You know all this."

"How about you fucking enlighten me?"

His lips pulled tight together, his posture tense at my proximity and the aggression I was displaying, filtering through the air between us in an unspoken challenge. Eyeing my wings, the muscles in his jaw tightened. He wanted to tell me so badly to fold them away so they were out of the prying eyes of humans, but he didn't want to create any more conflict than was already thick around us.

"Demons can be used as tools," he said, keeping his tone even as though he was explaining this to a child who should know better. I guess, in his mind, he was. "Sometimes a demon will cross paths with a human who's fated for death at that moment, and they will be killed. The demon will think it was a lapse of control, but it was no accident they were there at that time..." He paused. "Those humans were marked for death. Whether humans and demons believe in fate or not is irrelevant. They are fated to make choices, to be in a certain place at a certain time, that much is destiny, and the choice they make is up to them. But an out-of-control demon..." He shook his head. "If a demon kills a human outside of these circumstances, they will be sent back to Hell indefinitely or killed. In those cases, there's no lapse in control but a definitive choice." He eyed me. "That's the difference. The *choice* to kill. As you're doing now, making a choice."

I scoffed, and it was then he took a half step back from me, still not dropping my eye contact but a deep frown creasing his forehead. Zaqiel was growing angry. Good. Maybe if he lost a few layers of control, he might feel a snippet of the rage burning in me. Did he honestly believe everything that happened was part of some grand plan? Maybe it was all bullshit, just a cover to control us. Demons could get out of control like animals, but did that make it part of something greater? I doubted it. "But angels aren't tools..." he continued, taking another step back, "... we work *with* God. If we kill, we do so consciously and with spite against the system." His expression darkened. "We're *not* here to kill, Emrick."

When I spat at his feet, his eyes flashed, a smoky glow coming across them before they settled into the white of their natural form.

"I'm going to kill them. They deserve it," I said.

"That's not your call to make."

Zaqiel's wings unfurled with a loud whoosh after I shoved hard at his shoulders with my palms. I could feel my heart pounding against the inside of my ribcage, my breathing heavy and painful.

Every breath was painful now. There was so

much anger in me, I didn't know if I could stand it anymore. But killing those men and feeling their blood on my hands—no tools, I'd use my bare hands—that would help. I know it would. An eye for an eye, isn't that the saying?

They took her life, took her from me, so I shall take theirs.

"You are *not* to kill anyone," he said, his voice taking on the edge of our celestial tones. His warning was clear without saying too much—if he can't reason with me, he will stop me by force.

The problem was, we both knew if it came down to a physical confrontation, he'd lose.

Because he was still playing by the rules, rules I had thrown away when God denied me the act of revenge and murder which was rightly mine to undertake and allowed my innocent love to die.

"Fuck you."

"Those men will die when God wills it."

"I'm going to kill them." I growled as I closed the gap between us again. "I fucking *will it.*" Our wings came almost together, enclosing us in a cave of near darkness, the rain unable to break through the wall of feathers as we stared hard at each other.

"You'll fall," Zaqiel said, and if I didn't know better, I'd have thought there was regret or possibly sadness in his tone. But Zaqiel was on the side of right, and if I fell, he'd see it as what was *right.* Action and consequence. "He'll take your wings."

"I don't care anymore."

There was something in his eyes then, beyond the glowing white, and it was real pain.

"Emrick—" his voice was strained.

Shoving past him, I folded my wings against my back, and they disappeared from sight as I shouldered him. When I reached the street, I turned, taking what was likely to be the last look at my brother I'd ever have. His eyes had returned to deep blue, and he stood there, drenched from the rain but not feeling the cold, his wings folded away as he watched me make my final choice as an angel before I'd be condemned to fall.

"One day you'll understand..." I said. "And on that day, come find me, and we'll be brothers again."

It was done, and I'd be lying if I said I wasn't fucking glad about it.

But the consequences happened much faster than I had anticipated, and no matter how much I paraded in front of Zaqiel, beating my chest and claiming I didn't care and was ready to accept whatever befell me, when it happened, it hurt.

Never have I felt pain like it.

Waking up in an alleyway, it was still raining, and it was a wonder I managed to sleep at all, given the cold and wet. It was more likely that I passed out rather than had a nice, relaxing nap. After killing those men, and after the street had run red with their blood and it was washed down the drain in the downpour, I felt weak. Like something was taken from inside me, a black hole opening up in my soul and widening until it sucked all the energy from me. The rush I had felt when I wrapped my fingers around their necks, snapping them with a satisfying crack or simply tearing them apart with strength beyond their understanding, I felt invigorated at the time. But afterward, I was an empty shell. I had managed to stumble a few blocks before collapsing behind a dumpster, and while I slept, the rain had washed the blood from my hands.

Mostly.

When I woke, the searing hot pain stabbed through every nerve on my back, and a part of me was missing. Did I lose consciousness as some small mercy to not bear witness to their removal? To feel the blade of wrath slice down my back, severing my wings from me and condemning me to one of the fallen. I was spared that anguish, but the residual pain was just as bad, and now there were a thousand smaller shots stabbing into nerves where they had been.

My wings were gone.

I had not anticipated the emptiness of losing that part of myself. While I howled against the wind and rain, and my cries echoed onto the street as darkness ebbed around me, underneath the pain was anger at the injustice. Having done the right thing and removed those men from a world where they didn't deserve to live, I was the one to be forever punished.

So be it.

Pushing myself to my feet, I growled as my clothes rubbed against the raw and fresh scars on my back. Despite my curiosity and the part of my mind that just *had to know* what the damage looked like, I didn't want to see it. I never wanted to look upon those scars and be reminded of God's betrayal. He protects demons instead of angels, the out-of-control animals from below rather than the loyal who do his good work, and his precious humans, no matter how cruel they are.

The sunrise was at least an hour off, but that was okay, I had a decent walk ahead of me. I needed to get to her, but she never wanted to live in the city with her sister and had found a place in the suburbs. It didn't bother me before, but now I wonder if maybe she had convinced her sister, Emily, to leave the city, Emily would still be alive.

Without my wings, it would take hours to reach her on foot.

What did it matter? I had nowhere else to be.

There were no thoughts running through my mind as I walked, no pondering of the greater meaning of life or stopping to smell the roses—no such desire was left in me. There was only pain and anger, the latter masking the former, and I didn't want to feel the pain anymore, so I let the anger become a part of me to fill the void where my wings had been until it was all I had.

It was still early morning when I reached her home and pushed open the small white gate before I crossed the generous front yard, ducking under the tree branches dripping cool water from the now-cleared rain.

Knocking, I waited, and when she answered the door, her hair was messy and she was wearing a pink bathrobe, which she clutched closer to her chest when she saw me.

"Emrick," she said sleepily. "What are you doing here?"

"It's over."

"What's over? What are you talking about?" Her eyes were slowly widening as she woke further, and when she let her gaze trail over my body, my clothes damp and remnants of blood splatters still visible, she gasped. "Oh, Emrick." I could barely stand the combination of sympathy and terror in her voice. It wasn't necessary. "What did you do?"

Impulsive Emrick, rebellious Emrick. She was already assuming the worst.

No point in lying about it, I came here to tell her. "I killed them," I said.

"Are you out of your *mind?*"

"Alison—"

She cut me off, the anger in her voice crushing the plead in mine. I needed her to understand. "Why would you do that?" she cried.

"I did it for Emily and everyone like her. I did it for you, for everyone, so you're safe now."

"Emrick, you have no idea the powers you're dealing with. You've only made it worse."

"*You* have no idea the powers I'm capable of dealing with," I muttered.

Anger was bubbling beneath my skin, working its way up through the pit of my stomach. I didn't understand why she was acting like this. I had done the right thing—they were bad men who did bad things. Why was everyone so sure these men deserved to live?

"Alison..." I tried to reason with her again, the weight of everything was crushing my shoulders. There was no doubt in me I had done the right thing, but I thought Alison, of all people, would understand and would be on my side. I had done what she couldn't, but what I knew she wished she could. I had avenged her sister, taken the men who had taken her life. "They took her from me."

"They took her from *all of us,* Emrick. This was never just about you."

"They didn't deserve to live."

"You can't just go taking these things into your own hands!" she cried. When she threw her hands up in frustration, her robe opened slightly, revealing her nudity beneath. I was too angry to even be distracted by it.

"I thought you would understand."

Alison shook her head, curls falling from the messy knot on top of her head to cover her face as she clutched her robe closed again. "I can't condone this. Why did you come here to tell me?"

"You have no idea what it cost me to do this. I did the right thing."

"I'm sorry, Emrick, I don't think you did."

"Are you going to turn me in?"

She hesitated. "No."

I believed her.

We stared at each other for a moment, Alison drawing her robe around her further when the chill from the breeze passed over the porch.

"They didn't deserve to live," I repeated. "They took Emily away from us. It wasn't her time."

Alison shook her head sadly, her hand poised on the door. "Goodbye, Emrick."

The door closed with a gentle click, and I stared at the stained-glass panels. Even after a minute, I didn't hear any retreating footsteps. Alison was waiting just behind the door, perhaps wanting to make sure I left.

So, I was the bad guy? So, I did the wrong thing by taking an eye for an eye?

I was darkness, anger, and violence.

If that's all I was to everyone, then that's all I would be.

CHAPTER
1

EMRICK

Now...

No matter how much I had, I always wanted more.

My empire had grown over the years, and I was well on my way to running almost half of this city's underground crime network. Maybe I could have put my efforts into politics, becoming the mayor and moving up from there, but it seemed a waste of time. The real power lay within these not-so-secret networks which existed under everyone's noses. All citizens knew they were here, even the cops, but it was too big now, and drugs and prostitution ran this city, so I simply took my slice.

Then worked my way toward owning the whole damn city.

Because this was what I was good at, this is *all* I

was good at. I wanted people to grovel at my feet, for everyone who said it wasn't for me to decide who lived and died to realize they were at my mercy. They may have been right, but now I had that power, I owned it, and I *could* make that decision if I wanted to.

They feared me, my name, and everyone who worked for me. Using anger, fear, and hatred coupled with having nothing left to lose, I had carved out a section of the world I could control and claimed it as my own, doing what was necessary to retain and grow my empire.

There was nothing inside me now except the darkness—an empty void where my soul used to reside. I don't regret anything I did—regret is for the weak. Those men deserved to die, the first humans I had killed, and it was my right to take their lives. But afterward, I had no purpose, no direction, and found myself wandering the city getting into trouble, taking my rage out on anyone who looked at me wrong.

Until I found the club.

Urban was one of the largest nightclubs in the city, and now it was *my* nightclub, the place from where I ran most of my business. The second I walked through those doors almost a decade ago, it felt like a second chance. I could almost feel the power throbbing from the place—the combination of rich fucks and people who would do anything for a buck intrigued me.

I wanted it, all of it.

At the time, I had already formed a small group compiled of men working underneath me and made some cash through drugs, but the taste of power had me wanting more. Every fearful look I received from people satiated the black space inside me only a little bit, and I needed *more.* I'd like to say I had started as a bartender and worked my way up through the ranks or I'd saved money and bought the place, a real motivational story.

If I can do it, you can too!

But no, and my lips curled into a sneer when I thought about it. I had simply offered the owner a choice—the club or his life and the lives of his family. Once he had lost two fingers and an ear, I think he understood that I meant business. He'd shot me, but it didn't stop me from coming at him, and from there, he had argued no more, signing over the club, staff, and consequently, his share in the world of crime. He had spent decades building up an empire, and wasn't keen to let it go. Murphy was a tough fucker, and I respected him for it.

But I was stronger, faster, and had nothing to lose.

How he expected to stay in his position with a weakness that was a family—a family which could be threatened or murdered—was beyond me. The one weak spot I had was already taken from me, ironically, by Murphy's men. If I had known who he was when I took his business from him, he wouldn't have lived beyond my office door. It didn't take long to find his button, his weak spot, and while his reputation had preceded him as much as mine does now, he didn't want his children to meet me.

Don't blame him. Smart man.

Anyone with an ounce of logic knows you don't get into work like this if you have something to lose. Without any connections, I'm unplugged from the world, nothing to fear, and that makes me dangerous to my enemies.

Once I realized the connection between Emily and Murphy, I sought to kill him.

But someone had beaten me to it.

I had a good suspicion about who, but I didn't care enough about Murphy to look into it further.

That was eight years ago, after ending my self-destructive binge once I fell and decided to focus my energies. I lost my wings, so what more could He do to me now? Fuck all. God barely controlled me as an angel, and as one of the fallen, I was beyond His reach.

I'd lost everything, everything I loved and held dear as well as the bond with my brothers and sisters. When I woke up the morning after the act with my wings gone and large permanent scars on my back, something in me changed. Whatever was left of the angel vanished at that moment, and any loyalty or faith I had was gone. I was new—not better, much worse, in fact—I was different.

When there's no going back, you only look toward the next day.

Those fucking scars, scars that no matter how many times I tried to get them tattooed over, no matter how much I yelled at the tattoo artist to press harder, they would simply not take the ink. I'd be forever left with the reminder of my falling, and I supposed bitterly, that was the point.

Mostly my empire ran itself, and I only needed to intervene when shit hit the fan to remind them who was in charge and make sure through fear there was still power. Otherwise, I was free to engage in whatever I wanted. While I was mortal now, I retained my celestial strength, and from what I could judge from my slow, almost unperceivable aging, a certain level of extended lifespan. I'd even retained most of my accelerated healing abilities. Although I noticed as time went by, it took longer for me to heal, part of the punishment for murder, I guessed.

How this was supposed to teach me not to murder, I didn't know. I'd fallen as far as I could go, so what's to stop me from continuing to kill?

Slowly, I was becoming mortal, the time it was taking for the process to complete was a small mercy. One day I would die, so I might as well make the most of it.

My chosen pleasure for tonight lay under me on her stomach, squirming against the binds holding her wrists behind her back and the ties that clamped her ankles together.

Helpless. Beautiful.

Her once pale white ass was now dappled red from my punishment, and her whimpers and cries had taken on an edge which wasn't there when she first came to my bedroom.

Willingly, of course.

There was never force. I could charm with the best of them, and part of the sport lay in knowing they would eventually come to me. I could witness the conflict of fear and arousal from them and play with it and their minds until they submitted and came to my bed.

But I always warned them.

I might hurt you.

Yet the promise of pleasure, the forbidden, and unknown from a *bad boy* was a strong and irresistible pull for humans.

This one was just about at her breaking point.

Right where I wanted her.

She knew who I was, my reputation, but still she came to me willingly, without fear.

Well, maybe a little bit of fear. She'd be foolish not to fear me.

I'd encouraged her to loosen up with something to drink before we started, and we'd sat together in silence, sipping vodka, the creak of the leather couch under my fingers gained her attention every time I gripped it in my impatience. My cock ached against my pants as I watched her lick the liquid from her lips, so delicate. She was a tiny thing, barely five foot three and a waist size God knows what. Almost *too* small, I felt like I was going to break her when I threw her onto the mattress. But she'd proven herself to me, and I knew she was ready for more.

She hadn't come yet. I hadn't allowed it, and tying her hands had been a desperate measure when she couldn't keep her fingers off her clit, no matter how many times I told her she didn't have permission. I'd use her name to scold her, but I couldn't remember what the fuck it was. I'd been calling her *baby girl*, and she seemed to like that, mewing and squirming every time I dropped my voice and growled something into her ear.

Flipping her over, her eyes were brimming with tears, her cheeks flushed with humiliation and pain, and her hair which had been so perfectly combed into a ponytail had fallen out of the tie, and the ends stuck to the sweat on her forehead and neck.

Perfection.

"You've been a bad girl…" I hummed, smirking when she whimpered as I crawled over her, "… but you took your punishment so good, I think you deserve a reward."

Kneeling on the bed, I lifted her hips, and without another word, I penetrated her. I knew she'd be wet for me, and she didn't disappoint. As I leaned across her, I almost folded her over, her legs pushed back toward her chest as I pounded into her and slapped my hand over her mouth when she started screaming. I didn't care if people in the club downstairs or my men outside the door heard her screams, but the way her eyes widened with lust when I handled her roughly was ecstasy.

She was screaming with pleasure, and I wondered how long it'd last before she begged me to stop. They all did, eventually, when their bodies grew exhausted from the orgasms. I wanted them to come, to have that pleasure, but I wanted to get them there my way.

I needed that power.

She'd been begging for it, literally begging, and as fun as teasing and punishing her was, it was my turn now. I'd use her pussy until I came, then I'd torture her at the meeting of pleasure and pain until I was ready to go again.

These men and women I took, none of them lasted long in the job. I know the bar managers downstairs were growing tired of having to hire new people every time one of them quit, which they always did after a night with me. They thought they could take it, but none of them could, not for as long as I needed or wanted them to. They'd leave in the early morning hours when it was still dark out, marked by my hands and teeth and their thighs dripping with my cum and theirs, and they'd never come back.

When I was close to my peak, I thumbed her clit, forcing an orgasm from her, wanting to feel her clamp around me so I could continue pushing into her and past her resistance. I had to remove my hand from her mouth to make her come, and fuck, she was so *loud*.

I'd punish her for that too.

She was in for a long night.

CHAPTER 2

CARA

Who did he think he was?

Of course, I *knew* who he was, everyone did. Emrick—the man who owned the club, Urban, and as a fun little side project, also ran half the underground crime in the city. Everyone was in his pocket—police, politicians, pimps, distributors, small-time thugs, and their customers.

He ran the whole damn lot.

So, why any sane person would wonder, would I want to work at such a place?

Quite simply—money.

Many high-rollers patronized Urban, the sort of people who would tip ten times what I would have received for a night of dancing at the club a few blocks over. Of course, there were risks, but you needed to weigh those up when deciding about changing jobs.

Pro—money is better.

Con—occasionally, the club gets shot up.

In defense of my decision, it had been over two years since the last attack directly on Urban, and most people knew better than to go straight to the source of power. Although a little over a year ago, there had been a smattering of attacks on other bars, clubs, and buildings owned by Emrick. But there were also arson attacks on those owned by his competitors, and they seemed to have stopped as abruptly as they started.

These happenings probably shouldn't be public knowledge, but things had a way of getting around in this city, especially when it came to power struggles within the crime world. It was best to know who was on top so you knew where to tread carefully.

Hint—tread carefully everywhere.

I had gathered information from the girls at Urban as well as acquaintances working at other places that were an integral part of the nightlife, and strung all the snippets together to know more than I should.

Another good rule to abide by—*keep your damn mouth shut.*

I got my foot in the door at Urban to be a waitress and bartender through my friend, Maddie, whom I'd grown up with. It was time to earn some tips and bonuses, and I didn't even have to get naked to do it. I had no issue with my body, but I'd rather be in control of who saw it if I could, and while the strip club, The Palace, was a good place to make money, a job where I could keep my clothes on was better, especially if I made even *more* doing it.

Only once had I broken my rule about sleeping with patrons from The Palace, and it was fucking worth it. The man was a goddamn animal in bed and somehow managed to wear out three other girls and me on the same night. The next morning, he'd unceremoniously kicked us from his penthouse apartment, shouting for us to *get out* without moving himself, which somewhat cheapened the experience. But then again, I was hardly expecting him to ask me out on a date following an orgy. Shy wasn't a word I'd attach to myself, although ask my friends from high school, and they certainly would—shy Cara, innocent Cara. But they didn't know the truth of the things I had seen and done, and while I kept it tucked so deep inside for years, I barely spoke a word to anyone but Maddie.

Since then, I've accepted the darkness in me. I was messed up, and while I could try not to be, what was the point? Accepting that part of myself was liberating and only awakened further by that wild night. Something ignited the darkest part of me, and I looked back at my past with new insight with every year that passed. I had made mistakes, done things I'd give anything—including my life—to take back. But every step I'd taken since then had made me, and I wasn't shy or quiet Cara anymore. I was a force to be reckoned with in an unassuming body.

All this simply reinforced my mundane life in this city was pointless and wasn't making me happy anymore.

I wondered if it ever did make me happy.

So, while I had no debt and wasn't in trouble with any loan sharks, I needed the money.

Because I needed to get out of this city as far and as fast as I could. To make as much cash as possible the only way I knew how, given I was unskilled and didn't have much of an education to speak of. The schools in the city weren't exactly known for their scholars and graduate opportunities, and the opportunities which did exist were limited when everyone was going for the same few available. It's either who you know or who you're willing to sleep with.

If you were at the wrong end of the city, like Maddie and me, you were basically screwed anyway. Look out for yourself, never fully trust anyone.

God, it sounded worse than it was. We had good times, but my friendship and loyalty didn't extend to not getting the hell out of dodge when I could.

This brought me to Urban. I wanted money, *needed* money, to save as much as I could, get out of here, and buy myself a new identity and life.

No one would come looking for me. Then I could be whoever I wanted, and while I wasn't sure who that was yet, it had to be better than bouncing around between jobs here. Maybe I'd finally find my place in this world, a place where there were other people with darkness in them like mine, and I didn't have to pretend.

A place where the gun under my pillow felt more like a toy and less like a necessity.

Every corner of this city reminded me of the small pocket of my life I'd rather forget.

The memories were so strong, I couldn't escape them, and they haunted me. Behind the bright smile was an understanding that with the darkness came a monster, a monster who lived and breathed inside me and wanted me to let it take over.

Maybe with a new name in a new place, I could forget.

Maybe.

Emrick sat up there on the balcony overlooking the club and dance floor the entire night of my first shift, wearing sunglasses no less as if he were some kind of celebrity. I wondered if he did it every night, and if he was looking for anyone in particular or simply observing. Or perhaps it was an intimidation tactic to remind the occupants he was present and not to be messed with.

Then my mind wandered, and I wondered what

his voice sounded like and if all the stories I'd heard about the things he'd done were true. There was something terrifying and exhilarating about being even this close to a man like him. He had his shit figured out. He was a dark man, that much I knew, but he was *unapologetically* dark. He didn't try to hide it under false pretenses and didn't try to fit into the world which rejected him. From what I heard, if he needed to take a life, he did, and that was that— no second-guessing, simply business.

Some messed-up part of me envied him. He'd found freedom in the darkest place.

Being this close, both via my employment and now physically, while terrifying and exhilarating, another word swirled around in my mind, knocking into the others like bumper cars and reminding me to be smart.

Dangerous.

I needed to keep my head down and work as many hours as they would let me have, then get out, find my own place where I could be unapologetically me—darkness, monsters, and all.

It hadn't escaped my attention that wondering too much about a man like Emrick could land me in trouble.

Keep your mouth shut and *don't ask questions.*

Everyone knew who he was, and he was instantly recognizable by his sheer presence alone. With his height and build, coupled with the dark tribal tattoos snaking around his arms and neck, there was no hiding. So, why did he wear the sunglasses? What purpose did they serve?

He was an unreadable force, a blank slate which radiated power and danger and nothing more, no hint of personality or weakness beyond his extremely intimidating aura. Perhaps that was part of what allured him to wearing sunglasses. What I could see of his expression around the dark frames was blank. Emrick simply sat in that red chair on the balcony, his chin resting on his fingertips, watching, like it was his job to watch.

I was forced to turn away from staring at Emrick when one of the bouncers shoved past me, knocking into my shoulder and not slowing down when I stumbled.

Whatever.

Emrick wasn't my concern. I was here to make cash.

I had my own internal demons to deal with. I didn't need to know his too.

"Does he always do that?"

A week since my first night, and every night I was

there, so was Emrick on the balcony, watching over the crowd, barely moving and sipping vodka. Sometimes he'd have visitors, business I assumed, but he wouldn't acknowledge them more than he needed to, leaving most of the talking to the tall blond man who moved around the club a lot more than Emrick did. His righthand man, I guessed.

Maddie followed my gaze to the balcony, clicking her tongue to gain my attention when I kept staring. "Stay away from him," she said.

"I was just wondering—"

"This is not the place to be wondering about anyone, Cara. You know that as well as I. We both grew up in this city, we know the score."

"But—"

"Drop it."

When I glanced at the balcony again, Emrick's head was turned, and I'd swear he was looking right at me, but it was impossible to tell for sure. Maddie made a hissing sound between her teeth, and I faced her again.

"Stay away from him," she whispered. "If he comes near you, run."

"Why?"

"Fuck, girl, how did you survive in The Palace? You can't possibly be that naïve."

I shrugged. "I didn't have to worry much at The Palace. I had Carl." A smile crept on my face at the memory of him—intimidating to look at, but one of the sweetest men you could ever meet. He looked out for all the girls there. Being a bouncer was more than a job to him—we were his second family.

Maddie was loading glasses and a bottle of rum onto a tray for me, and she rolled her eyes, followed by an understanding nod. "There are no big bouncers here with a heart of gold who will protect you, girl. These men work for Emrick and Emrick alone. This is a dangerous place, I told you all this before you started."

"I'm just curious."

"God, how can you be so blasé about the threat he poses? Don't be *curious*..." She punctuated the word with air quotes. "Don't ask. Don't look. Fuck. Men like him deserve to be..." Maddie shook her head, sliding the tray across the bar and snatching at my wrist when I went to lift it. "The only thing you need to know is this. Since I've been here, several of the bar staff have been invited to have a drink with Emrick, and every single one of them quit the next day."

Something dropped in the pit of my stomach, and desperately I worked against the desire to turn around and see if Emrick was still looking at me. I felt as though he was, as if he knew we were talking about him, and the gaze behind those glasses was still boring into the back of my neck. Part of me wished he'd stop, and the other part wanted to stare him down to see who would look away first. If

I took up the battle of wills with him, if it came to his darkness versus mine, I wondered who would come out on top?

I remembered the shape of his arms.

I wouldn't mind if he were on top of me, though.

Internally, I groaned. That sounded lame, even in my head.

"What did he do to them?" I whispered. My curiosity was mingled with an inkling of fear, and I knew the fear should be winning, that I should be scared enough of Emrick and the threat he posed to look away and keep my head down indefinitely. It was fun to imagine the darkness behind someone's eyes, to write a tale in your mind about who they might be beyond the rumors. But faced with the reality of who this man was, my stomach churned.

Was that because I was afraid? Or because I wasn't and knew I should be?

Emrick had embraced his darkness, made a life out of it, but no light was left in him. I may have had darkness of my own, but it was nothing compared to the man on that balcony.

"I don't know what he did," Maddie said, letting go of my wrist and helping me balance the tray, "But maybe we shouldn't be too curious to find out, don't you think?"

Dark Angel

Less than two weeks, that's how long I was at Urban before he came for me. I cursed under my breath when he entered the kitchen—there was no way he didn't know I was alone in there. Busying myself washing the champagne glasses, I kept my eyes down to the sink and simply hoped he was looking for someone else and came in here by accident.

But I knew better. No one else was here, and I doubted someone like Emrick would go *anywhere* by accident or for a lovely stroll.

It was the first time I had seen him come down from the balcony, and I trembled as he stood across the steel counter, staring at me. He stood unnaturally still, his chest and arms a solid barrier. I didn't look up, and the sound of glass against glass in the sink wasn't enough to drown out my heart pounding in my ears.

His presence was suffocating me, and it was almost a physical strain not to look at him now, not to challenge him with a stare, daring him to look away first. I cursed my curiosity. I simply *had* to keep looking at him, didn't I? I just couldn't keep my eyes from straying to the balcony, and every now and then, I'd catch him looking right back at me, and

I never looked away fast enough. Sometimes I even let my gaze linger, and we'd pause like that for a moment, simply looking at each other, a silent communication over the club's noise.

Perhaps like recognizes like. His darkness reflecting mine.

Maybe he was simply checking me out.

Dammit.

Emrick said nothing and started drumming his fingers on the steel bench. I allowed myself the smallest sideways glance at his hand, taking a moment to study the hints of his tattoos peeking out the sleeve of his hoodie. All his men wore suits or long jackets, but Emrick was almost always in a hoodie. I supposed when you had his sort of power, you could wear whatever you wanted.

That was hardly important right now, and I almost forgot to breathe when he stalked around the U-bend of the counter and came to a stop behind me.

Immediately behind me. So close I could feel my ass brushing against the fabric of his pants.

"Hello."

His voice was so deep it sounded like it should belong to a sex god.

Maybe it did.

Shaking my head and holding back a tremble in my shoulders, I dared not turn around but found I couldn't continue washing glasses either. Frozen on the spot, my hands hovered over the sink. Maddie's warning about being too close to him was screaming in my mind.

Run.

Dangerous.

But I was trapped against the counter.

Where could I run to?

And the intrusive thought, reminding me of who I really was—*would I run, even if I had the chance?*

Emrick was electric against me. I wanted to lean back against him, imagining those fingers that had drummed impatiently against the counter running over my body.

No.

All the things I had heard about Emrick had made him something dark and mysterious—a forbidden temptation, a curiosity, the cryptic figure on the balcony who I could project my messed-up fantasies onto. His dark image was amplified as the warnings I should have listened to screamed and rattled around inside my head.

He had a reputation.

Murderer.

Pure and simple.

Although me, of all people, should know it's never that black and white.

Emrick removed people who got in his way on his rise to the top. Rumors of ex-employees being dropped off buildings, people losing fingers for stealing, even of someone being literally branded a thief as though Emrick got the inspiration for his punishments and messages from medieval times.

Then there was what Maddie had told me about young men and women invited to his office for a drink, and whatever happened traumatized them so much, they never came back.

Or maybe they were simply never seen again.

"Hello, Mr. ... sir," I stuttered when I realized I didn't know his last name.

He chuckled, a deep rumble in his chest, and I felt his breath against my neck and had to work to suppress another shudder. I couldn't be seen as weak in the eyes of a man like this, or I'd become a victim. Ideally, I wanted to fly under the radar and blend in with everyone else in the club. But my stupid curious butt meant it was too late for that now. My gaze was drawn to him every night I was on the floor, and now I knew he had been watching me too. I had brought this attention on myself.

God, he was so sexy, heat was practically radiating from him, and as much as I wanted to tell myself my shudders were purely based in fear because I knew that's how I *should* be feeling, my truthful voice reminded me they were mostly due to something else.

Arousal.

"Just call me Emrick," he muttered.

"Is there something I can help you with, Emrick?"

He chuckled again, and I had to bite my tongue to fight the embarrassment building in my throat, constricting it. I had intended for it to sound like an employee asking a simple question, but instead, the words were so breathy I might as well have asked if he wanted a blow job.

"Am I making you uncomfortable?" he whispered.

Emrick shifted against me, and I pressed forward into the counter, desperate to limit the contact with him. His body was hard, a solid force between me and any escape, his build and height while striking from a distance, was downright intimidating this close.

Too close.

Don't get turned on, I told myself desperately, willing it to be true.

Because the reality was, the combination of danger and power *did* turn me on, and for the most messed-up reason. A reason I had been running from for years.

Am I uncomfortable?

No.

Do it more.

"Yes," I whispered.

Lies.

And he knew it.

Another puff of air against my neck, like he was huffing out a silent laugh at my discomfort, or perhaps because he knew I was lying. His hands found my waist, and the way his palms rested in the curve above my hips and fingers splayed across my exposed midriff made me feel particularly small and vulnerable.

Carl would never let this shit fly. He'd protect me from Emrick and from myself. But Carl wasn't here.

None of the bouncers here would protect me. They all worked for Emrick.

"How about now?" he asked. His dark voice barely more than a whisper, but it didn't need to be. Beyond the thumping of the bass from the dance floor, muffled by the twisting hall leading to the kitchen, the room was empty and silent. I was so attuned to him, I swear I could hear his blood pumping through his veins. He pressed his hips against me, and I scrunched my eyes closed, gnawing my lip and biting back the moan that threatened to escape. He was hard. But he was dangerous, and this was a dangerous situation. I needed him to leave.

"Please." I swallowed, my mouth dry.

Stop.

Keep going.

What was wrong with me? I know what those hands had done, the orders those lips had given, and no level of physical attraction was worth risking my safety. I needed this job, I needed the money, and I didn't want whatever happened to the others to happen to me.

I didn't want to risk liking it.

I'd left The Palace for this place and didn't want to go crawling back after only two weeks.

Emrick's chuckle was cut off as the door swung open, and immediately he broke contact, taking a step back from me. I took a grateful breath as my space was clear of his presence and finally dared to turn to look at him. But while my eyes were shimmering in tears of frustration I couldn't contain, his expression was blank, unreadable behind the dark sunglasses.

The man who had come in with a tray of glasses stopped dead at the sight of Emrick, immediately staring at the floor and not even daring to stutter through an apology. I prayed he didn't turn and leave, leaving me alone with Emrick again. Because all I could think was how the bench was a perfect height to sit on and be screwed by the incredible hunk standing next to me. But Emrick flicked his hood over his head and shoved his hands in his pockets as he stalked out of the kitchen. When I released a heavy sigh, the waiter looked at me, and we made brief but pained eye contact. He said nothing, and I didn't expect him to.

He didn't ask if it was consensual, if he had stopped something from happening, or simply come in after it already had. He had a job to protect as well, and no one questioned Emrick.

CHAPTER

3

EMRICK

She would be the next, there was no doubt about it.

No matter how hard she tried, she couldn't stop herself from looking up at me as I watched over the club from the balcony. And I could tell she was trying, those quick glances she cast up and then just as quickly looked away. Several times a night, every night. If she thought she was being subtle, she was mistaken. Tate had noticed her, too, and running his fingers through his spiked white-blond hair, he slumped on the couch next to my chair.

"Who is she?" I asked.

"Cara. She started a couple of weeks ago. One of Maddie's friends, apparently."

"Maddie?" The name didn't ring a bell, but then again, I didn't often bother to learn the names of employees who didn't do my dirty work. The bar and waitstaff were of little interest to me, a necessity to keep the club running and extra cash coming in.

That, and providing easy pickings when I felt like a fuck and was too lazy to look elsewhere.

Which was often.

They knew who I was here, and I liked how they feared my power.

No one came to work at Urban not having heard something about me, I was sure. My reputation had spread across this city faster than my territory grew and helped pave the way when I wanted to take those areas over. How many of the rumored stories were true? Well, probably most of them. But stories had a way of getting twisted. My favorite tale was I had bitten off a woman's finger when she rejected my marriage proposal. That story amused me. It was a ridiculous premise.

I'd never get married.

Smirking, I drummed my fingers on my chin. *But how did they know I liked to bite?*

Fear was a powerful tool in control, so I never denied nor corrected these rumors, and simply let them flourish and do the work for me. The more people who were afraid, the less likely they'd come in here and try to claim my territory from me.

Because if I had to protect what was mine I would, at any cost.

Human life meant less to me than it should

because it had been shown to me they were all pawns in God's game, destined to live and die as He said. This city had proven itself time and time again it wasn't worth saving and even when you tried to help, the people didn't want it. All the rich fucks down at one end, looking out from their penthouse apartments over the parklands, ignoring—or pretending to, at least—the trash down this side. Here, the people would turn to crime for the smallest offer of money—turn on their friends and family, maybe even take the life of another human. What kind of world was that to save?

When I was a Watcher like my brother, I thought I could help them.

But not anymore.

Now I'm one of the fallen, and this is where I belong.

Whenever I missed my brothers and sisters, I'd simply fuck the rage away. My chosen human may be worse for wear, but I wouldn't kill them, as they had done nothing to me to deserve death at my hand. They'd be pleasured, even if the pleasure was mingled with pain.

They never came back, and although I always promised next time I'd be gentler, there was never a next time.

It wasn't a promise I could keep anyway.

"Maddie's been here for a year or so, good worker."

"Good." I was barely listening.

It wasn't as though I would go around killing people without regard. I'd have to be pushed to my limit before I took that step. They had to *deserve* it and have proved to me they weren't worthy of life. I was no demon to be placed in a position by God and used to rid the Earth of those ready to die. As an angel, even a fallen angel, I couldn't be used that way.

Thankfully.

Cara. I muttered the name under my breath. It felt good wrapped around my tongue, and I suspected she would too. But her curiosity seemed to evaporate when we were alone together, and she practically shivered when I stood behind her in the kitchen.

She was afraid, and I wondered what she'd heard.

That part made me angry. I needed only the right people to fear me—the worst of the worst, those like me. But not the innocent. A bit of fear was fun, but the fear which brought tears to her eyes and had her frozen on the spot, like she thought I was going to snap her neck right there in the kitchen, boiled the rage inside me and ignited something else.

Although, there was something about her, as though behind her tremble of fear there was a hint of arousal, maybe something I could bring out of her.

Something she was afraid I *would* bring out in her.

She smelled so fucking good, and I sneered—there was definitely arousal there.

I couldn't promise I'd be gentle with her, I never was—a rough touch built from years of rage burning within me and never seemed to fade. The mingling of pleasure and pain was too good to deny me in the bedroom. But none left unsatisfied, and they all came to me willingly, leaving only after multiple orgasms and dripping in fluids.

Having a human body underneath me was the ultimate power. Earthly pleasures felt so fucking good—I've not found anything to replace them, not drugs nor violence. Nothing topped the feeling of someone trembling with bliss under me after being pushed to the edge of their tolerance, their pussy or ass pulsing around my cock as they came.

Fuck.

Tate pretended not to notice as I shifted, hiding my growing erection from him. He'd been with me from the early days, and getting hard while watching Cara certainly wasn't the most compromising position he had caught me in. But he remained stoic and unreadable, which was fine. I hardly wanted to talk feelings with him. All I needed to know I learned from his work ethic. Tate came to me lost, wandering the streets, and betrayed, and

I'd given him purpose, honed his skills and anger into a fine point that could be aimed where I needed him most. Trust was only built over time, and we'd taken down enough common enemies for him to be my number two.

We also shared a common hatred for demons.

But I'd never trust Tate completely.

I trusted no one that thoroughly.

He understood that, and I'm sure he felt the same. If it came down to him or me, I wouldn't hesitate.

Tate's scars told me a story I needn't ask him about—a bonding between human and demon torn apart and how he had become who he was. I knew those scars, born from a severed bonding they were unique and recognizable. I knew what they meant, but I had never asked about his past, about the demon he had apparently once loved, much as he never asked about mine. Men like Tate and me, we didn't talk about the darkest recesses of our pasts but moved forward, always forward. Each day that ended no longer mattered, and only the next one was important.

I'd deal with Cara later because when there was a knock on the door and Sven stepped in from the stairwell, I could tell by his face it was bad news.

There was business to be dealt with.

"I told you this would come back at you."

Tate stared at me, judgment on his face. He had never liked Ray, and I didn't blame him. When I hired her as part of my team to take care of some of my more violent warnings—messages to deliver via broken bones—I didn't like her either. But she was strong, fast, and craved the security only I could offer. She was a lost demon looking for a path and the freedom to do her demon shit—fucking and fighting—without consequence. I offered her that, and she pounced on it.

But one night she took off, and I hadn't seen her since. Although I had kept tabs on her, she'd be stupid to think she could leave my employ without consequence. She wasn't worth my time then, but I knew one day I'd need her again and would need to know where to find her.

Tate had warned me then as he was reminding me now, that letting her go without punishment for her abandonment and her previous actions would come back and bite me in the ass.

And as one of my clubs—Darkside—on the south end went up in flames, Tate was convinced it was her, and Sven agreed, although he knew better than to speak his opinion in my presence. No one but Tate could get away with talking to me like that. Sometimes his condescending tone grated against me, but he didn't do it often, and I knew it came from a place of loyalty. But in those times, I wished more than others I still had my wings and could unfurl them, let my eyes glow white, and show him what real power was.

Remind him that despite our working history, he should always be afraid of me.

More than once, I had considered taking him to the bedroom to remind him who was boss—he looked like a fighter.

"Do you still know where she is?" I asked, ignoring the meaningful looks the two were casting each other, their thoughts as clear as though I could read them—*we should have killed her last time.*

"Of course we do," Sven grumbled.

Standing, I zipped up my hoodie. "So, let's go get her."

CHAPTER
4

EMRICK

Tate came with me as I suspected he would. I figured he was hoping I'd allow him to kill her. Any chance to kill a demon, and he'd be thrilled, no doubt projecting the face of his ex-bonded partner onto them. But that wasn't my intention, not tonight. I hadn't even come armed with what I'd need to completely destroy her. Yet I had my strength, which should be enough to warn her.

Like a child, Tate practically pouted as I told him to wait outside the apartment building, and twisting the door handle, I shouldered my way into the foyer, the lock giving way. It was dark out, but I wouldn't have cared if it were the middle of the day. Those who recognized me wouldn't dare try to stop me, and those who didn't, it would only take one look to make them back off. If they wouldn't back off, well, I was looking for a patsy to take my frustration out on.

Stepping off the elevator, I strode toward her apartment door, placing my thumb over the peephole and knocking. My shoulders tensed when there was mumbling and giggling behind the door, my fingers clenching and unclenching. I could smell the bitch, fucking demons stink to angels, and the rage bubbled in my stomach at the memory of what she had done.

A year ago, I had let her shit go on longer than I should have because she wasn't only targeting *my* buildings, they were random attacks, and I assumed it was some kids being fuckheads and playing with fire, literally. But then Ray strolled straight through my front door, and everything fell into place.

Until one night, without a word, she left.

If she thought that would be the end of it, and I'd just give up and not keep tabs on her, she was mistaken. Typical arrogant fucking demon. She was nothing more than a time bomb, waiting on the sidelines until I needed her skills.

That was until she decided to start fucking with my business again.

The lock turned with a click, and I was pleased to note she didn't bother having one of those little useless chains. I shouldered the door the second the latch was released, reaching through the gap and grabbing a handful of her red hair, forcing her to her knees.

"We meet again, Ray."

Her eyes flashed yellow, and I grinned. I *wanted* her to turn into her demon form, and my look simply dared her to do it. *Give me a reason to kill you.* She hadn't screamed when I grabbed her, only grunted as she was forced to the floor, her hands on my wrist as my fingers were next to her scalp, tangled in her hair.

Pain ignited in my other arm, and I spun, keeping my hold on Ray to find her partner's—Ilsa, a human—teeth driving into my skin, drawing blood. With a roar of rage, I threw Ilsa from me, staring at her when her eyes also flashed the bright yellow of demonic power.

"You bonded, how sweet," I hummed. "Now you've got something to lose."

Ray said nothing but continued to fight against my grip on her hair. When she couldn't budge it, she hissed at me before spitting out, "What the fuck do you want, Emrick?"

She continued to struggle, so I leaned in close and whispered in her ear, "Stop struggling, or I'll make a ring of your girlfriend's blood and torture you while you're powerless." Immediately she stopped moving, her eyes widening for only a moment before she glared at me. Demons had weaknesses, and even unbonded, the blood of the one a demon loved was a powerful tool and could be used as a trap to weaken and stop a demon from taking their true form.

I'd be able to torture her without her fighting back, and she'd have to watch Ilsa bleed.

"You're up to your old tricks again…" I growled out, tugging on her hair, "… and it's going to stop *now*."

"I don't know what the fuck you're talking about."

Ilsa ran at me again, leaping onto my back. I slammed her against the wall, crushing her between the wall and me. The corner of my lip twitched when I felt the plaster crack behind her with the force of the impact. Ray screamed as she was dragged sideways. Ilsa grunted but didn't let me go and began clawing at my eyes.

"For fuck's sake!" I bellowed.

Letting go of Ray, I reached over my head and grabbed Ilsa's T-shirt, bending and pulling her over my shoulders before slamming her onto the floor. With a boot on her chest, she clawed at me through my pants. I ignored her.

When Ray went to attack me, I held a finger out at her. "You touch me, and I'll crush her ribcage into her heart." Ray hissed at me, but I knew she was well aware I had the strength to do it. Bonded or not, Ilsa was still human and could die like one.

"Tell me what you want, Emrick." There was no resignation in Ray's voice, only rage. "You come into my home and attack us. What. Do. You. Want?"

"You burned down one of my buildings *again*. I thought we had an understanding."

"I didn't do shit."

Scoffing, I chuckled. "Who else would it be, Ray? It's your calling card."

"Probably one of the many fuckers you piss off every day. I don't care, and it's not my problem."

"You walked out on me. Did you think I'd just let that go? You owe me, and one day I'll be coming to collect. But I didn't think you'd be stupid enough to attack my territory again."

"I didn't do anything!" she screamed.

There was a banging from upstairs as though someone was hitting the floor to protest the noise we were making. Ray rolled her eyes and her shoulders to calm her stance.

"Emrick," her voice was calm now. "It's not me."

Lifting my boot from Ilsa's chest, she rolled out from underneath me and jumped to her feet, placing herself firmly between Ray and me.

Stupid woman.

"I saw myself in you when I first saw you with her. You connected with a human." I stared at Ray, my gaze flickering for a moment to Ilsa. "But I don't believe you didn't do it. You're still just a *demon*." Eyeing them both, my fingers twitched with the need to teach them a lesson, simply for being a demon and a human weak enough to love one if nothing else. Do I give her the benefit of the doubt? It would be foolish, and Tate would never let me hear the end of it. It would seem like a weak move.

Tucking my fingers, I used the base of my palm to slam into Ilsa's face. She cried out as blood exploded from her nose before she dropped to her knees. It would be easier to hurt her than Ray and would also send Ray a strong message.

You have something to lose.

Ray screamed in rage and fell to her knees next to Ilsa, touching her shoulders and hair, whispering comfort while Ilsa glared at me through her fingers.

"If it happens again… one more fucking time…" I held a finger up menacingly, "… I'm coming for you."

I left.

Taking the stairs three at a time, I needed to expel some of the energy that had built inside me, and the elevator car felt too small and confined. Perhaps I'd try to get Cara to come to me again when I got back.

Tate was waiting where I left him and raised his eyebrows in silent question as we began the short walk back to Urban.

"She claims not to know anything about it," I said.

"Of course, she fucking does."

Humming my acknowledgment, I watched Tate closely for reaction as I said, "She might not be lying. She seemed to genuinely not know why I was there."

Tate scoffed. "Demons are good at lying."

He was right, so I didn't argue, and while his face told me everything I needed to know about just how much he disagreed with my actions, he said nothing. I felt restless, and my shoulders and fingers twitched as we neared the club. I had denied myself something by not injuring or killing Ray, if for nothing else than all the trouble she caused me last year, and now the energy was trapped within my body.

I needed release.

I needed Cara to come to me.

CHAPTER
5

CARA

The club was winding down for the night by the time they got back. Emrick had stormed out of the building, the rage almost visibly flowing from him, and it felt as though it was an omen that someone was going to die tonight. While I didn't want anyone to die—unnecessarily at least—I found myself hoping Emrick achieved whatever he set out to do, partly because I didn't want him angry when he got back, and also because, for some reason, I wanted him to be happy. Emrick hardly struck me as the sort of man who would deal well with not getting what he wanted.

Wiping down the bar near the deserted dance floor, I was getting ready for closing and was one of the few still working. Being the only one behind the bar hadn't bothered me until I felt his presence.

What did he want with me?

I could only guess.

"I'm sorry I scared you the other day."

My eyes flicked up at his face as Emrick approached, leaning his forearms on the bar, and I guess trying to look sincere behind the sunglasses, but he was twitching, his fingers clenching and releasing. I was about to begin wondering again why he always wore sunglasses when he took them off. He kept his head tilted down toward the bar as he gracefully slid them off his face and folded them up, placing them delicately in his pocket. My hand stayed frozen in place on the bar where I had been cleaning it, my breath caught in my throat as I waited for him to look at me.

I'm not even sure why I was holding my breath. Perhaps it was the feeling I was about to get a glimpse of the man behind the mask, and coupled with the query as to *why* he'd show me whatever he was hiding, I was wondering what I'd see.

I wasn't prepared for the darkness.

His irises were so dark, they were almost black. I've never seen anything like it, and it was as hypnotizing as it was terrifying. I understood why he wore the glasses—he looked like a man possessed. Although the effect was both striking and chilling, he could use it to his advantage.

Emrick held my eye contact for as long as I dared to look at him before I cleared my throat and continued cleaning. This had been a good week, and I had made a decent amount in tips, adding it to the stash in my apartment. Opting to keep the cash in a shoe box under my bed rather than put it in a bank, it would make it easier to simply leave when I wanted to.

Pressing my lips together, I nodded but didn't trust myself to speak. He screamed danger, but when I cast him a nervous glance every few seconds, it was hard not to notice how strikingly handsome he was. Those eyes coupled with his dark hair—as usual pulled into a low ponytail—and the tattoos that snaked their way around his arms and shoulders, ending at his hands and, from what I could see, covering his chest too, he was goddam gorgeous.

Emrick wasn't the sort of man you wanted to be attracted to, and my constant awareness of what he was capable of kept me on edge.

He was drumming his fingers on the bar. He often seemed to be filled with energy, always moving his fingers or hands. He was either still as a statue or fidgeting and shifting, there was no in-between. Despite everything, he was my boss, and I didn't want to stop working and stand there staring at him, so I continued cleaning. As I neared him with the cleaning cloth, no longer able to keep up the pretense that only the other end of the bar needed a wipe down, he snatched at my wrist. He was so incredibly fast, I dropped the rag in surprise before immediately yanking away from him on instinct.

"Don't pull away. Please."

Please.

It was a command, not a plea.

His fingers gripped and flexed on my wrist, and I kept myself angled away from him, casting my gaze around for someone, anyone who could break his attention from me.

What did he want with me?

The voices and warnings of Maddie and the other girls rang in my ears, but there was something so intoxicating about his eyes. His expression darkened when I stopped pulling away from him, but I didn't move any nearer either.

"Come here."

Before I knew what I was doing, I had stepped toward him. One single step had me pressed up against the side of the bar, my arm stretched across the mahogany as he maintained his grip on my wrist. When he snaked his other hand around the back of my neck and pulled my face toward his, I stiffened again. He stopped when we were no more than an inch apart, and I could feel the brush of his breath on my cheek.

There was something about him, and I cursed myself for getting this close.

Despite everything—growing up in this city and witnessing all the stupid things people do, not to mention the stupid stuff *I've* done—there was always a part of me that felt I was somehow invincible and could look after myself no matter what. My childhood and life experiences had been nothing compared to what I knew others in this city suffered, although the whole thing exploded in my face with a few messed-up acts.

Call it stupidity because I sure did, but there was a tiny hint of lingering faith that deep down, most people were good. Because whenever I needed someone, whenever I was in the gutter and reaching up blindly, someone would take my hand and help me, even if only for a moment. I never drowned in this city like many do, but I was afraid I would, which is another reason I had to leave. This place had a way of chewing people up and spitting them out, leaving them as a husk of their former selves or bringing out the worst in them and displaying it to the world.

I didn't want the world to see the worst of me, not again.

When I saw Emrick's eyes, there was something there beyond the darkness—a broken man who had so much anger he directed it at anyone who stood in his way. But I wondered if with a gentle touch, I could show him not everyone was bad.

I wondered if his anger was masking something else.

I was kidding myself.

All the things I had heard about him, all the warnings and stories, this wasn't a man with some kindness lurking within him. I had acknowledged to myself he was unapologetically dark, and there wasn't any coming back from that.

But there was the other side of the coin. If he was as dark and rough as everyone said he was, then my God, he had the potential to be excellent in bed.

If he didn't kill me.

Emrick's breathing hitched as my fear spiked with that final thought. When his fingers tensed around the back of my neck, the vulnerability of this position came rushing to me in an instant. I couldn't believe I had given him this much power and put myself in a place where he had all the leverage. Being in a semi-public place wouldn't save me, not with him, not when he owned it. No one would dare question or stop him, even if I was kicking and screaming.

But I wouldn't. I already knew I'd go willingly, jogging after him like an eager puppy wanting a treat. He had me. It was obvious with how I wondered about him and couldn't seem to accept he was as bad as everyone said, even though he literally had blood on the hand that held me.

I was already his, but I hadn't admitted it yet.

He leaned in further, his dark eyes flickering between mine, wide and green.

"Don't be afraid of me," he whispered against

my lips.

I swallowed, and it felt heavy. "It's hard not to be." Raw honesty. I'm not sure if it was the best course of action, but I barely had the frame of mind to think of anything else I could say to this man. "But..." I couldn't get the words out, the admission he turned me on as much as he terrified me would seem too real if I were to vocalize it.

The chemistry where he touched me was burning into my skin, but my mind and body were screaming conflicting messages at me—all the stories I had heard were swirling around in my mind. Was he *too* dark? Would he be the mistake I couldn't, or didn't, come back from?

The one-night stand, the orgy, with the man from The Palace, had been mind-blowing, the best sex of my life, and the tingle between my thighs and the electricity passing between us told me Emrick could be better—the best. Between him and I, something incredible could happen. But was he *too* far gone? Would I be in genuine danger in his bedroom?

Whatever happened, they never came back.

He interrupted my thoughts with a deep growl. "I could make you feel so fucking good, Cara."

My legs just about gave out when he said my name, and part of me was surprised he even knew it. Emrick radiated power and drew me to him like a magnet. It was too much, and I couldn't resist.

If Maddie were here, she'd stop me.

She would save me.

I hated I was glad she wasn't here.

His fingers tangled into my hair at the base of my skull, holding me in place but not pulling me any closer to him. However, we couldn't possibly get any closer than this without kissing.

"Come upstairs," he said. The breathy whisper was gone, and the words were somewhere between a command and a request.

My lip began to tremble as I fought internally.

Go.

Don't.

Dammit! You need this job.

He growled again, deep in his throat, and I trembled.

"I can't."

His thumb started rubbing against my wrist before he traced his fingers up my arm, a gentle touch in stark contrast to his grip on my neck. "Come upstairs."

No, I couldn't. I needed this job. I needed to be away from this city because nothing but distance would spare me from the memories which haunted this place. No matter how incredible it was, a one-night stand wasn't worth the risk. Funny how my mind was totally ignoring the risk of *who* he was and what he was capable of. What does that say about me? All I was thinking of was the stash of

money under my bed—my out from this place—
and the reminder that others who had gone before
me hadn't returned.

Something in his expression changed when I
tried to pull away from him as his fingers closed
around my neck. Abruptly, he let me go, and I
stumbled back against the other side of the bar, not
even aware I had been pulling so hard against his
hold.

Emrick watched me as I straightened, pulling my
skirt down and fidgeting with my top, unable to tear
my eyes from his and biting my lip in indecision. I
knew I had made the right choice in not going with
him, so why did it feel like I was in trouble for doing
something wrong?

Because I *was* in trouble.

I was his. I just hadn't admitted it yet.

He tapped his fingers on the bar impatiently, and
when he slid his sunglasses back on, I couldn't read
his expression anymore, as if the sunglasses acted
as a blanket, shading out his thoughts. Was it anger
or simply frustration?

While he didn't look back as he stalked off, I
knew this wasn't over.

CHAPTER
6

EMRICK

Cara didn't come to me last night, but that wasn't a good enough reason for me to stop trying. Because I felt the hesitation in her. The electricity that passed between us was hard to ignore, and the excitement that flared in her eyes when I touched her only surged me forward. They didn't always come to me easily, but they always came in the end. Plenty of women who attended the club regularly were practically screaming for a fuck. I could take any of them, but it would be pointless. I needed someone with resistance and fight. I needed someone who was a challenge because it made the victory sweeter. There was no arousal when someone threw themselves at me on a dance floor, grinding obscenely against my leg or groin.

It was too easy.

Humanity hadn't endeared itself to me much over the years, so I enjoyed the hunt.

Cara was ready for me. I simply needed her to admit it to herself. Her internal fight was useless, and she'd eventually crumble at my feet.

Adjusting in my seat again, I sighed loudly as my cock strained against my pants. I was alone tonight, save for the nameless guard at the door to the balcony stairs. Sven and Tate were off sorting out a watch for Ray's apartment and visiting my other venues to ensure they were on high alert and security was increased.

Thinking about Ray surged a flush of anger through me. The anger lived right below the surface of my skin and came out at the smallest provocation. It had never died, not in the decade since I fell. The darkness never subsided, and I had never accepted my punishment. Because the injustice still grated against me, and it would forever more. It was easy to grip onto the anger and let it fuel me.

Snapping my fingers, the guard lifted his chin.

"Vodka," I said, and as he turned to leave, I snapped my fingers again, pointing off the balcony once I had his attention. "And I want *her* to bring it to me."

He nodded, I turned back to the dance floor, waiting for him to emerge from the bottom of the stairs and watching as he moved through the crowd. They parted for him, the crowd closing over the empty space as soon as he had passed through. It was mesmerizing the way people moved with the music as if they were one mindless organism. As though music somehow connected them to a part of the world beyond their understanding.

Perhaps that's why people sing in church. *He* does like that.

Maybe not this music, though barely discernible over the bass. Rubbish.

Cara glanced up at me as she loaded a tray with a bottle of vodka and a glass and followed the guard toward the stairs. I had plenty of vodka in my office, but she didn't need to know that.

After letting her in the door, the guard nodded at me and closed it behind him. He knew enough to wait outside, but the move set Cara on edge. Her back straightened, and she bit her bottom lip, glancing nervously between me and the closed door behind her.

Nodding at me, she sashayed over, placed the tray on the table, and unloaded the bottle and glass. Before she had stood fully, I said, "Sit." Cara stared at me for a beat without moving, still bent over after placing down the glass, her cleavage on display. She saw me looking and bit her lip again, straightening and clearing her throat quietly. "Why don't you take a seat?" I said again, trying to soften my tone.

It wasn't easy. I much preferred to command.

She nodded stiffly again before sitting on the far end of the couch away from me. Lifting the glass, I swirled the contents, watching her while I took a sip and licked the liquid from my lips, the burn so sweet. She shuddered, and my lip twitched. Almost a grin.

"Relax."

"I'm relaxed," she snapped.

"We don't have to do anything tonight."

Cara glared at me. "What makes you think we're going to *do* anything at all?" she drawled.

I laughed then, a low rumble in my throat, and took another sip of my vodka. "Seriously, Cara, just fucking relax, will you?"

She glared at me for a moment longer and then sighed, sinking back into the couch and crossing her legs, making her skirt ride up over her thigh and offering me a nice view. We sat in silence for a short while before she finally tired of it. "Why am I here?"

"I wanted your company."

"Why? You don't even know me."

"Maybe I'll ask your friend all about you."

She scoffed. "She doesn't really know me."

That wasn't the reaction I expected. Most girls gush over their friends or get defensive of me mentioning them at all. Jealousy was ugly and rampant, but Cara brushed the words aside as though her friend was nothing. "Oh really?" I asked.

Cara's lip twitched. I thought she was going to

smirk. "I've known her for a long time, but the person I am with her... it's not really me, not the darker me. Besides, all she cares about is money, and she can be a bit judgmental..." There was a pause, and when she started talking again, her tone changed. "But maybe she's just like that because she cares."

I watched her. It was almost as though she let her real thoughts slip, then caught herself before she got too far into a monologue. She needed to talk, and I wanted her to talk to me.

I wanted to know about this *dark side* of her personality she mentioned.

Removing my glasses, I folded them and placed them in my pocket. Leaning forward, I rested my chin on my fist before saying, "You say I don't know you, so tell me about you."

A deep frown etched on her forehead as though she was trying to figure me out. I was *dangerous*, the one who everyone feared. So why was I being nice to her? She'd be wondering why was I even talking to her.

Call it luring her into a false sense of security.

But she was smarter than that, and she wasn't buying it, and as far as she was concerned, she had already let too much slip. Others might stare at me suspiciously for a moment, but once they got talking, they would relax. Most people liked to talk about themselves. They would tell you they'd learned from this city not to talk too much, but given the opportunity, they'd spill their whole damn sob story or just talk shit for twenty minutes straight. Humans weren't as smart as they thought themselves to be. That's why I was in this position and not them, and why they clung to those who held the power, because, deep down, they knew they weren't cut out for it.

But Cara remained tight-lipped, figuratively, and literally pressing her lips together. The suspicion in her features made me chuckle again.

"How's your night been?" I tried again.

She laughed at my question. It wasn't cruel laughter, not at my expense as such, but she understood the absurdity of my asking. "Lovely, dear, how was your day at work?"

Grinning, I took another drink. "Very satisfying."

"Kill anyone today?"

My smile dropped, and she pursed her lips, her expression triumphant. She shifted uncomfortably when I stood before dropping heavily onto the couch, taking pleasure in how she jumped before I slid across to be next to her.

"You think you're so smart, don't you?" I growled.

She lifted her chin in defiance, but there was fear in her eyes at my proximity. Would I hurt her? Kill her? She didn't know me well enough to know. I was a dark anomaly, moving through this club and city and taking as I pleased, leaving a trail of stories of power and darkness in my wake.

"I'm smart enough to get out of this city as soon as I can."

Pulling away slightly, I studied her face. "You're leaving?"

"What do you care?"

Leaning in close, I brushed the hair from her shoulder, breathing in the scent of her shampoo and sighing against her ear. She trembled. "Because I haven't fucked you yet."

"I don't think that's a good idea," she whispered.

"I never said it was."

"But that's never stopped you before, right?"

I chuckled. "Right."

"I think I've done enough things I regret without adding another."

I sunk back into the couch next to her, and after a beat, she followed suit but kept her arms folded close over her chest so we weren't touching. She kept glancing at the door and back at me as though plotting her escape route. If she ran, I wouldn't give chase.

She'd come back.

"Tell me your story."

She laughed again, this one a breathy chuckle. "No, thank you."

"Tell me yours, and I'll tell you mine."

"I know yours," she said.

My face darkened. "No, you don't."

Staring at me for a beat longer, she sighed. "I can't trust myself here with you." When my eyebrows shot up, she stared at the ceiling as though looking at me would make this confession impossible. "I did some... things, some terrible things. Some I regret, some I don't. But they've left me..." she waved her hands over her body, "... messed-up."

"I like messed-up." She was intriguing me more by the second, and when she looked into my eyes, there was pain in hers. As I reached across to touch her arm, she jerked away from my hand. Anger flared inside me. She was treating me like I was goddamn poison, and while I knew I was, I didn't need the reminder from a human.

I needed to fuck her.

"Come to my bed."

"I can't."

"Yes, you can."

"Fine, I don't want to."

When she stood, I stood with her, closing the gap between us until her breasts were pressed against my chest. "That's a lie."

Her eyes widened, and she scanned my body. I could practically feel her legs weakening.

Oh yes, she'd be mine very soon.

I wasn't holding her against me, but she didn't move away, either. "You're the worst thing I could do right now. I know who I am inside, and I know who you are, and this…" she moved her hand between our faces, "… would be incredibly stupid. I might…"

"You might what?" She almost whimpered, and I lowered my face to her neck. I wanted to bite her throat and drag my mouth across her breasts before using my teeth on the other side of her neck. I wanted to mark her. "You might… *like it?*"

A whimper did escape her lips then, and something stirred in me while my cock twitched in my pants. I know she felt it. What was she afraid of? What was in her past that would make a difference if she let me fuck her?

"Why are you doing this to me?" she whispered.

I waited until she was looking into my eyes again. There was fear in her face, but now I suspected all her fear wasn't of me. Maybe she was afraid because she *wasn't* afraid and knew she should be. Perhaps she was darker inside than she was letting on.

She could be like me.

No. No one was like me.

Maybe the arousal and attraction were getting the better of her, and the logical part of her mind telling her this was a bad idea was losing the battle.

That was scaring her.

"I want to fuck you," I answered honestly because I didn't know what else to say. Initially, it was physical attraction to the foolish girl who started working for Urban and couldn't keep her eyes off me and keep her head down like a good girl should. The one who couldn't stop looking up at the balcony and wondering about me. Her curiosity got the better of her. But now, *now* it was different. Now *I* was curious about *her,* and I'm not the sort of man whose attention you wanted to gain. All I wanted was to peel back her layers and find out what she was hiding from me.

She scoffed, and looked away.

"Go." When I stepped away from her, she threw a tentative glance at me before looking at the door. I nodded. "Go." She looked back at me, and I growled. "Because I know you'll be back."

She squeaked, and I barked out a laugh before turning to sit and watch the club again, listening to the click of the door as she left and shuffled past the guard to move down the stairs.

She'd be back.

It had been so long since I had heard the rain that heavy. It pounded so hard against the street and buildings it was an impenetrable blanket, almost

impossible to see through. But I knew where to find her, where she always was at this time of the morning. I'd push the door open, the door she left unlocked for me, and the little bell above it would chime. She'd come trotting into the foyer, covered in flour, sugar, and fuck knows what else, and her face would simply light up *when she saw me. I'd never seen anything more beautiful than her smile, and for whatever reason, she felt I was worthy to receive it. She was beautiful—her short brown hair framed her face in a neat bob and lips she always kept ruby red framing teeth slightly too large for her face. How did I ever get so lucky as to gain the affection of a woman like her? When she'd skip across the linoleum—leaving a cloud of flour in her wake, she hugged me, giggling at the way the flour stuck to my clothes and hair—I couldn't help but stare at her. It pained me to know she didn't yet know the truth about me and my nature, but it didn't matter because when she looked at me, she saw someone worth loving.*

Love.

Something I had witnessed in humans, something I thought I knew. Love for my brothers and sisters, love for the human race. But that was nothing compared to the love I felt for her.

Emily.

The days started early for a baker, but she never complained. She loved it, loved her work.

She'd invested everything she had into that little bakery. Although the positioning was terrible, being right next door to a nightclub, her windows were often vandalized. Or she'd come to work at four in the morning to find someone pissing on the outside of her door, too drunk to realize what he was doing.

She threw herself into her business, and the community loved her.

I loved her.

When I first saw Emily, she was standing behind the counter, her smile lighting up the room more than the sunlight streaming through the large windows, the cursive gold writing casting small shadows on the floor. It was her first day owning the bakery, and I knew this because she told me. She was telling everyone who walked through that door, the little bell announcing their arrival.

The woman took my breath away. I'd been in this city too long, helping where I could, and seeing her was finally finding the light. I needed a reminder that sort of light existed in this world. I went back every day, and as we talked, she opened up to me. One day she made me a picnic—red and white checkered picnic blanket included, the cliché topped off by the large tree we sat under and Emily's blue dress cascaded over her legs as we sat. She tried new recipes and let me taste them first, the pastries melting with flavor in my mouth. They tasted almost as sweet as she did when her lips met mine.

As I approached the bakery through the rain, the skin on my back began to tingle, and my fingers twitched. My wings wanted to come out— they were pushing against me from the inside, desperate to be freed and to protect me from dangers yet unknown.

Something was wrong.

Emily!

A crack of thunder exploded, followed shortly by lightning that webbed its way across the clouds and lit up the night sky as I bolted toward the bakery, my boots splashing heavily in the puddles on the uneven road. My breathing was loud in my ear drums, and my heart pounded against the inside of my ribs. Every beat was painful, and the sense of dread which filled me only expanded as I neared until I felt I was going to explode.

The door was unlocked.

She always left it unlocked for me.

But not for them.

The little bell's chime sounded broken with the force I slammed the door open with, and when the door hit the stop, it was joined by another clap of thunder as I fell to my knees beside her lifeless body. Emily's blood was bright and red against the black and white floor, her hair messy with blood and brain matter from where the bullet had exploded out the back of her skull.

Howling, I threw myself over her beautiful body as the cavern opened up in my chest, my ribs pulled open and out as every ounce of love escaped and was replaced with a crushing grief saturating my soul. Through the hole that was now in my heart I'm certain my soul escaped, and my body sucked up all the darkness in this world, filling me with it until there was no more room left for anything else.

For what was there to live for if not her?

Through the decades, I had seen some terrible things.

But until now, I had never cried.

Pushing my hair out of my face with a sweep of my hand and over my forehead, I sobbed as the water dripped from my hair, mingling with the tears streaming down my cheeks.

I didn't know who they were, but they would pay for this.

"Emily?" I whispered.

I knew she was dead. A human soul could be sensed, felt. It radiated from them and shaped their nature and warmth. A soul would create a blanket of hazy color around a person angels could see if we focused, usually enhanced when they slept, when they were diving into their own subconscious and at one with the spirit world which existed only a veil away from their own.

But this body in front of me wasn't Emily.

She was already gone.

Her soul would be in Heaven—what a beautiful place for her. But I couldn't be there with her as I was here, and her life on Earth had been tragically cut short.

Did I ever tell her I loved her? I couldn't remember.

Touching her shoulder gently, I pulled her toward me until she rolled over, not even sure I wanted to see what was left of her face and have it forever imprinted in my mind. But I needed to know and be sure. What a pathetic hope to hold on to, that she was some doppelgänger and not really Emily, that Emily was hiding somewhere, waiting for me to find and rescue her.

When I rolled the body over, the eyes that stared open and wide at me were not the deep brown I knew, they were green, and the hair that lay bloody and messy on the floor, wasn't dark and straight but chestnut brown and wavy.

I choked out another sob. "Cara?"

The room was dark when I woke and snapped my eyes open. I didn't scream or move but simply laid staring at the canopy of my four-poster bed.

Sleep doesn't favor me, which is not normally an issue. I rarely sleep, perhaps every two or three days. But tonight, I needed it. I had been awake too long, and it was catching up with me.

But sleep wouldn't come again tonight, not now after those images.

The heavy curtains on the windows blocked out all the sunlight, and the room was suffocated in darkness. I had laid there for hours, and when sleep eventually came to me, I was haunted by nightmares.

What the fuck did these images mean? Emily was never far from my thoughts, although as every day passed by, her face became harder to recall. I wished I had a photograph of her to remind me why I was who I was and did what I did. I wanted to remember her face before it was blown apart.

Sentimental fool.

What's past is gone, and there's nothing I can do to change it.

So what does Cara have to do with this? I felt as though I had found a kindred spirit, drawn to each other through a suppressed darkness. Although, in my case, not so suppressed. There was no point in hiding my darkness because it was all I had now, and if I were going to be cast as the bad guy, then by God, I was going to run with that for all it was worth. *In for a penny* and all that shit. Maybe when I died, I'd go to Hell and could spend my days fighting off the demons I hated so much.

Cara.

If only for one night, I would have her.

The people I chose became my obsession, a game I played until I had them, claimed them, and made them my own. But Cara, she had infected me, and if she'd run away afterward like all the others had, then I'd have to take my chance to destroy her and ruin her for all other men.

Because the darkness she claimed was in her was nothing compared to what lay in me.

CHAPTER
7

CARA

"Where did you go?"

"Sorry?" I looked at Maddie, jumping when I felt the cool liquid of the beer overflow onto my fingers. "Dammit!" I hadn't been paying attention and hastily turned the tap off and poured the beer down the sink, shaking the excess from my hands. The customer raised his eyebrows as I apologized profusely, but I was thankful for the lift of his lip indicating his amusement at my blunder.

Handing him a fresh beer, I smiled. "Sorry about before, sir."

"That's okay, love," he drawled with an accent I couldn't place before winking and disappearing into the crowd.

Exhaling heavily, I swept past Maddie to rinse my hands.

"You disappeared for a second there." She glanced at my hands, smirking. "Obviously."

"Sorry, just thinking."

"About Emrick?" My hands paused, and I cleared my throat. When I turned to Maddie, she rolled her eyes. Any amusement in her expression had vanished, replaced with a look as hard as stone. "What the fuck, Cara?"

"I'm sorry! I can't stop thinking about him since he cornered me."

"Since he *what?*"

"Shit. Sorry, I didn't tell you."

"Tell me what, Cara? What happened?"

I held a finger up to her when a customer cleared her throat impatiently. I served her drink before returning to Maddie and assisted with wiping down the bar. Waiting for a lull after a particularly bass-heavy section of music, I said, "He cornered me in the kitchen when I was cleaning, then again when I was alone here at the bar, then he wanted to… *chat.*"

"What happened to *run?*"

"I dunno, Maddie, I just… froze."

And I was distracted by how good he smelled and how amazing his body is.

"All three times, Cara?" She was barely keeping her voice steady.

"Is there something I should know about you two?" I asked.

Maddie looked incredulous, her cheeks

reddening as though I had slapped her. I almost smiled at her reaction but was hesitant to prod her further. She looked on the verge of shouting at me in front of everyone, scolding me for being so stupid and careless as to get close to him. Biting my lip, I reminded myself Maddie had worked here longer than I had, and she had no doubt seen a lot of things in that time. She was only trying to protect me. After all, it wouldn't be the first time she had—she and her parents took me in even though they could barely feed Maddie when I had nowhere else to go. I should cut her some slack.

When I went through a self-destructive phase, she was always trying to bring me back, although I could tell her patience was wearing thin by the end. When I came to her from The Palace and asked if she could get me a job, she looked both relieved and worried at the same time—I suppose aware of this place's dangers but also the job's monetary benefits.

Although part of me was hesitant to let myself get as close to her as we were when we were kids because, after everything, I got this job specifically to get enough money to leave this city. While that would mean leaving Maddie behind, there was nothing else for me here but bad memories.

"He's dangerous!" Maddie hissed at me. "He deserves to die!"

"I know, I know. I'm sorry."

"Don't *apologize* to me, just stay away from him. I'm only here for the money, and I know are you too, but that man deserves nothing, *nothing* but death for all the things he's done. And that's only what we *know* about, Cara. Don't you see?"

"This city is full of messed-up people, Maddie."

"I know that, but he's the worst of the worst. People thought it was bad when Mr. Murphy was in charge, but Emrick took him down with *ease.*"

"What did he do?"

"Mr. Murphy lost two fingers, an ear, and his family was threatened. I don't think there's any doubt Emrick would have followed through with his threats. Then..." Maddie looked around, "... after Mr. Murphy signed everything over, he—"

"Do you wanna get back to work, girls?" Phillip, the bar manager, snapped at us.

"Sorry," I mumbled, pressing my lips together as I glanced at Maddie and left to serve the floor with an uneasy feeling in my stomach. What was it about Emrick that had gotten under my skin? Pure animal magnetism, I suspected. His body was *incredible,* and that was only the brief snippets I had seen. I knew that type of physicality should scare me more than most because of my past, but somewhere along the line, things had gotten so twisted in my head, the power now turned me on instead of repulsed me. But why it was overriding the logical side of my brain that knew this was a bad idea was beyond me. Maybe I should just sleep with him and get it out of my system.

But then the reminder would spring up in my mind of all those others who had walked in these footsteps and not come back after their night with him.

What did he do?

Maybe they simply couldn't handle him.

"Thank you," I said, throwing a customer a simpering smile as he slipped a hundred-dollar note onto the tray as a tip. Pretty average for the club, and really the only reason I was still here. My hands were full, and I couldn't secure the note, but the man smirked as he picked it up again and tucked it into my cleavage. I muttered another thank you, trying to keep the scathing in my voice to a minimum as he brushed his fingers along the top of my breasts completely unnecessarily.

It was times like this I wished the bouncer from The Palace was here. Carl wouldn't tolerate that shit.

When I turned, he slapped my ass, and I jumped at the unexpected contact, dropping the tray of glasses to the floor. The sound of the metal tray and the shattering glass garnered the attention of what felt like half the damn club.

"Damn," I mumbled as I dropped to my knees and started picking up pieces of glass and dropping them onto the tray.

"Let me help." The man took my hand as he kneeled beside me.

"Don't touch me," I snapped, angry and humiliated at the attention this was amassing and the nerve of him to touch me in the first place. This never happened at The Palace, and I hated that a place where I was required to get naked to make money was safer than being here serving drinks.

"Bitch, I'm just trying to help."

"I wouldn't need help if you'd kept your hands to yourself," I hissed at him.

The sound of his slap across my face rang in my ears, reverberating around the inside of my head even as I reached up and clutched my cheek, now stinging from the impact. I reacted on instinct—meet violence with violence—and curled my fingers slightly, slamming the base of my palm into his nose. He roared and recoiled before being yanked to his feet, blood spilling from his nostril as he fought against the men pulling him upright. I heard the click of heels behind me before I, too, was helped to my feet by two of the girls.

"Are you okay, sweetie?"

Rubbing my cheek gently, I hissed through my teeth again. "Yeah, I will be," I said to the waitress who came to help. I didn't know her name, and with the adrenaline surging through me at the coppery scent of his blood, I didn't care.

"Get him the fuck out of here!"

Silence.

Looking up, Emrick was leaning over the edge of the balcony, his knuckles white as he clenched the railing. His lip was lifted into a snarl, and my jaw dropped as the blanket of silence fell across the club, only the beating heart of the bass continued as everyone realized who was speaking.

Because Emrick never interfered with what went on in the club with the patrons, he couldn't care less as long as it didn't interfere with his business. I'm sure it wasn't the first time something like this had happened. Customers can get handsy, and I'd seen at least two fights break out since I started. The bouncers would tear them apart and throw them out, but there would never be a shout from Emrick like that. Loud and commanding, he had the attention of the entire place.

If this was some ploy to get me to go upstairs with him…

Well, it was kind of working.

Dangerous.

Dammit.

There was real fear in the eyes of the man who had hit me as he was dragged from the club, and I watched his progress across the dance floor, the heels of his shoes squeaking as he was pulled and my hand still resting on my tender cheek. Maddie came running, shifting my hand before touching the mark on my cheek and ushering me toward the bar.

"Can one of you please clean up the glass?" she called over her shoulder before sitting me down on the bar stool and reaching over the counter to wrap some ice in a dish towel and hold it against my face.

"Thanks, Maddie."

"You okay?"

"Yeah, I'm okay."

She sat opposite me, concern flooding her face as her brows furrowed and dabbed the ice against my cheek.

"At least it's good money, right?" I said, and she chuckled.

"Yeah, it's good money." Her smile dropped as I withdrew the note from between my breasts and slapped it onto the bar. Neither of us mentioned how Emrick had intervened. I didn't know what to think of it, and I doubted Maddie did either.

"You didn't have to hit him, Cara."

I snatched the ice from Maddie, holding it against my cheek. "Excuse me?"

"He's a good tipper."

"He *struck* me, Maddie." Her shoulder twitched as though she was going to shrug, and anger flared in my eyes. Some things weren't worth the money, and being smacked around by some arrogant rich guy was one of them.

Maddie pressed her lips into a thin line, then said, "Think we can get the rest of the night off?" She lifted her glance to Phillip, who let his eyes flicker from me to her before he nodded stiffly. "Fuck yeah, girls' night!" Maddie cried, and I smirked despite the ache in my cheek.

"Tequila, please, Phillip." I moved to slide the hundred-dollar note to him, but it was gone. Eyeing Maddie, she slid the note to him, crumpled from being gripped in her fist. My eyes narrowed, but I said nothing to her and looked at Phillip again, "And keep them coming until this is spent."

They didn't even try to hide it.

Hell, I knew they were bold, and that Emrick and therefore his men ran half this damn city, but Christ, I thought they would have made some effort to keep their business private.

Emrick strode back into the club after disappearing for hours, flanked by three of his men and with another less fortunate man under his arm. He struggled uselessly against Emrick's grip, clawing at his forearm as Emrick crushed him against his side in a headlock, practically dragging him through the club while he had no choice but to keep his feet moving so he wasn't being dragged by his neck alone. Emrick didn't look at him and barely seemed to acknowledge the man's weight, walking with the same purpose he always did.

I couldn't help but suck in a breath as they walked past, and when Emrick was close, he threw a glance at me. I couldn't see his eyes behind his sunglasses, but as usual, his expression was blank, lips turned down and pressed together in grim determination. His glance lingered longer than it needed to, and with my hand pressed against my chest, I could feel my heart drumming against my ribs. My fingers snaked up to my cheek where I had been struck earlier, and while I watched the fear in the man's eyes, I remembered the act of protectiveness Emrick had shown when I had been hurt.

What sort of man was Emrick really? I couldn't tell.

The stranger had stopped struggling and was now simply trying to keep up with Emrick's pace. His face was already bloody from a broken nose, and the only thought that went through my head was *I wonder what he did.*

There was no assumption in my mind Emrick was acting incorrectly, and my immediate reaction had been this man, whoever he was, must have done something to wrong the dark man who ran this club and this city.

Was that wrong of me? I'm sure it wasn't an incorrect assumption in the sense he must have done something, but exactly what he did was something I couldn't even speculate on. Emrick's business spanned from drugs to prostitution and simply from the clubs, and this man could've been involved in any of them. The lines of right and wrong were well beyond blurred when it came to how Emrick ran his business. Simply because this man had *wronged* Emrick, it didn't follow he had acted incorrectly or unlawfully. Hell, he may have even been acting on the side of the law or acting to protect his own best interests.

But then again, so was Emrick. He was protecting what was his.

I knew what that felt like.

Shaking my head and turning my back when Emrick finally looked away, I blamed the tequila. It had been much too long since Maddie and I had a night where we could chat and laugh, and despite Maddie telling me when I started that the bouncers wouldn't look out for me, somehow, it was now in my head Emrick *would*. He still scared the hell out of me, but he also ignited something in me, and my curiosity about him was far from abated.

If anything, it was awakened further.

Along with everyone else in the club, I turned my back and pretended to be oblivious to the man's struggles as he was dragged upstairs. Unwillingly, my gaze followed them as they crossed the balcony. Emrick was the last to enter the door beyond the balcony area, searching the dance floor until he came to me, staring for a beat longer before he disappeared and slammed the door behind him.

"Are you out of your fucking mind?" Maddie hissed at me.

"What did I do?"

"Christ, girl, come here so I can talk to you." Maddie grabbed my upper arm and dragged me around the corner of the bar, ducking under the hatch and stopping near the trap door to the cellar. "Staring at him like that, what's wrong with you? You know as well as I do you ignore shit like that. Christ, Cara, when I offered you a job here, I thought you knew better. How many times do we need to go over this? This is exactly what I was talking about. You haven't seen half the shit I have here."

"Sorry, I—" I stopped myself. *Why was I apologizing to her?*

One of the bartenders emerged from the trap door, carrying a few bottles of vintage wine. He arched an eyebrow at us but seemed otherwise disinterested in our conversation as Maddie dropped her grip on my arm.

"You survive in places like this by keeping your eyes down and your shit to yourself."

"I know."

"You can't trust anyone, Cara."

Frowning at her, I nodded, stopping when my head started spinning, the tequila had hit hard when I stood. When her hand flew out and grabbed my chin, forcing me to look at her, I grimaced.

How did she know I was about to look up at the balcony?

"Just keep to yourself, okay? You look out for *you*. That's all everyone here does."

"Including you?"

Maddie sighed heavily. "You know that includes me. We're friends, but in this city, in the end, it's everyone for themselves. Money and freedom trump almost everything in places like this."

She was right, and while I knew it, it still sucked. Despite our night of giggles and fun, and even though we grew up together, I knew if it came down to it, it was so engrained in both of us to drop everything and look out for number one, and neither of us would hesitate if we were put in that position. Had I even considered Maddie in my plans to leave? No. I'd miss her, of course, but my goal was about me and nobody else.

Here, it was everyone for themselves.

That meant Emrick too.

So, whatever his plan was when he helped me tonight, whatever he wanted with me, it was about him.

And I think I needed to be reminded of that.

CHAPTER
8

EMRICK

He had witnessed the arson attack on my club, or so I was told. It was enough for me to demand he be brought in, and in a bout of anger, I had decided I'd go with them to bring him back. Cara's hesitancy to come to me had built my frustration, and my hands ached with how I kept clenching my fists. I needed to release this anger somehow. It wasn't unusual for it to take a bit of convincing to get the women or men to come to me, but they all did. Eventually.

But *her*, she made my fingers tingle whenever I touched her. The way the goose bumps exploded over her skin where I ran my fingers up her arm or across her stomach, she was so fucking responsive, even if she wasn't aware she was doing it. She needed some rough play. Her face and body were screaming for it, even if her mind was sending her messages otherwise. Even if her smartass mouth was protecting her, while her mind told her it was a bad idea to come to me, her body, and at least part of her, was aching to let me take her.

She'd come to me.

But for now—business.

Shoving him into a chair, he grunted under the impact and sat dutifully still as cable ties were used to bind his wrists and ankles.

"What's your name?" I barked.

"E... Eli." He had stuttered but recovered himself. The squeak left his voice and was replaced with a deeper tone, which I'm certain was fake.

"What was your business at Darkside, Eli?"

Darkside was the club that had gone up in flames.

"I was just getting a drink," he said.

The sound of my palm colliding with his cheek ricocheted around the room. None of my men flinched, and I wouldn't expect them to. They had seen much worse than a simple slap across the face.

"What was your business at Darkside?" I repeated, mercifully giving him a moment to recover and straighten his back.

Eli coughed, no doubt covering a much less masculine sound of pain. "I was just... getting a drink."

This time when I hit him, he went down. A backhand across his other cheek sent the chair he was tied to tipping over, and his shoulder collided with the floor, the soft carpet doing nothing to soften the sting of the blow. When he coughed again, blood and a tooth fell on the floor, and I rolled my eyes.

I should have put plastic down. I'd have to get one of the guys to deal with the stain later.

"Sven, get some plastic to put under this fucker's chair. I don't want blood on my carpet."

Sven nodded as Eli's eyes followed him desperately. "Wait, please!"

"What was your business at Darkside?"

"I was scalping business, okay! Selling drugs."

"That's my territory, Eli." I kept my tone even, finding cool indifference to a human's suffering was always more effective in growing their fear than responding with anger ever was.

"I know. *I know,* I'm sorry. The customer base is so good."

"I know it is. I spent years making it that way. People want drugs, they come to my establishments... that's no accident." Leaning forward, I placed my hands on his forearms, letting my weight rest there and bringing my face close to his. "And you thought you could come in and take off the top of all my hard work?"

"I'm sorry, please."

"You're a handsome man, Eli."

His pupils darted between the lenses of my glasses. I'll bet he could see his own pale face reflected in them before he looked at each of the men around the room, unsure how to respond.

"I—"

"Maybe there's something you can do to make it up to me."

He trembled. I know he knew what I meant, and it was no accident the insinuation was there in my words. Yet when I had finished punishing him, I imagined he'd *wish* it had come down to me taking him to my bed.

"Please."

Honestly, I expected him to say *anything, I'll do anything.* I liked it when people offered to do *anything* to make up for their mistakes, even if those mistakes had been made with intent. Because I liked to watch their eyes widen when they realized that *anything* might be worse than they imagined. *Anything* might be harder to take than they had hoped.

Eli cried out when—with a boot between his knees—I broke the chair, forcing my weight down until the wooden legs gave way, and his legs spread out in front of him. He continued to shout as I smashed the chair around him until only broken slats of wood were bound to his wrists and legs, but he was otherwise free, surrounded by the pieces of his former prison. The chair was by no means sturdy or expensive, but it still took particularly well-aimed force and strength to break it like that—

something I had honed to perfection over the years. Humans had a way of imagining their head and body being in place of an inanimate object broken in front of them.

Pinning Eli to the floor, I crawled on top of him while he continued to look desperately at my men. Their expressions would be as stoic as mine, half of them I'm sure were staring disinterestedly at a wall. While they'd seen worse than what I was doing now, they'd never been in the room when I was fucking someone.

I wasn't into voyeurism.

My men had no real need to watch every move I made while interrogating, they were only here to make sure Eli didn't make a run for it, and, of course, the intimidation of having them here helped.

But Eli was mine to do with as I pleased.

"Eli," I whispered. With my hands on either side of his head, I moved my lips close to his and leaned over him, poised on all fours—a ridiculous position for someone like me to be in, and yet, it worked. He was stiff as a board lying under me, terror at the very real possibility of what was to follow flowing through him. But beyond the fear was something else, an insignificant speck of arousal, of curiosity which piqued at my proximity. I could smell it on him. He was thinking about what it would feel like to be taken by me, penetrated by me. I asked him again, "What did you see that night?"

I knew he was out back doing a deal when the fire started, and he knew I knew. He must have seen something. Cameras show three people running out the back door while the rest of the staff and patrons exited through the front and onto the street. No one was killed, that's why I suspected Ray, she destroyed places but she never killed. I needed to tie her to this.

"Three men," he whispered frantically.

Shit.

"Not women?"

"No, no. Three men running out after the fire started."

"Can you describe them?"

"Yes, one was—"

"Not to me, Eli. You'll tell my men after."

His eyes widened. "After?"

Pulling back, I kneeled over him, and Eli remained lying stiffly on the floor, unsure what to do. I lifted his left hand and kissed the top of it, hovering my lips over the skin. He trembled.

Well, might as well make a rumor true while I'm here.

"Eli, will you marry me?"

"W... what?"

Gasping quietly, I placed a hand dramatically on my chest. "Did you hear that, boys? He rejected my proposal."

There was a general snickering. They knew the stories and could guess what was coming next.

Removing my glasses, I stared at him with eyes almost black, letting my voice take on the same darkness. "Stay out of my territory, Eli."

Eli started pleading again as I took his ring finger between my teeth, almost down to the knuckle, and Sven stepped over, kneeling on Eli's shoulders and slapping a hand over his mouth as he began to struggle.

We all knew the story.

He rejected my proposal.

So, I took his finger.

"Have they moved?"

"No, they haven't left the apartment."

Grinding my teeth, I stared at the mirror behind the bar, the bottles reflected along with my dark expression. Eli had given me little helpful information, and it was getting harder to contain myself. The men he had described tearfully, cradling his bloody hand, had no recognizable tattoos and wore no gang colors or biker cuts. Their eyes were a human brown, not a demon yellow, and nothing about their appearance would help me track them or link them to any of my rivals. They had known where the cameras were, and there was no sign of their faces.

Eli turned out to be useless.

Still, he wouldn't be selling in my territory again, and my reputation was strengthened. The cloud of fear which surrounded me and shifted people to the side on the odd occasion I walked through the club was larger.

Good.

"Keep watching them," I said.

"Yes, sir."

Ending the call with my thumb, I tossed it onto the desk. The big flashy desk wasn't to my taste, but it seemed pointless to spend money redecorating an office I hardly used. Besides, I somewhat liked the idea that Mr. Murphy *knew,* for a while at least, that I was sitting at this stupidly big desk which *he* chose in *his* office decorated like art deco was still in fashion. I was more hands-on rather than purely sitting behind a desk and having others do the dirty work for me.

Mostly.

Although from what I heard, my predecessor had made no secret of his own violent tendencies, and I'm certain more than one person was killed in this very office.

But the watch I had put on Ray's apartment, I

was happy to outsource to one of my men further down the ranks. I wanted to know every move that bitch made, and when she stepped out of line again, we'd be there to take her down.

Then I could take her down *permanently*.

Because I was still certain she was up to something, although Ray wasn't the sort to outsource her bullshit and would do things herself. The men Eli had seen were not carrying anything that would have lit the fire and could have simply been patrons escaping. But every chance at information had to be taken, no matter how slim, and I hated that now all I could do was wait for the culprit—Ray—to make another move.

The night hours passed slowly, and I moved out onto the balcony to watch the crowd moving around in the club, the numbers increasing until the place was a big ball of sweat and pheromones as people sought out the high of their choice—drugs, alcohol, sex. Although there was the occasional exchange of cash and drugs going on, I'm not sure why they bothered to try to hide it in a handshake, given most of the drugs they were selling came from my labs anyway. Everyone knew better than to sell other products within my club. Even with the sleight of hand, I could catch a glimpse of the black angel wings that marked my products' packets.

Yes, I chose the symbol for the irony.

I'd been told my cut of cocaine even had its own

name—*Dark Angel.*

I liked it.

But this shit with Ray had highlighted something for me—I had gotten lax, taking for granted my territory was mine. I didn't act when one of my major labs a few hours out of the city was massacred many moons ago, and I didn't act straight away when Ray burned down a couple of my buildings last year. I told myself it was because she wasn't focusing only on *my* buildings, and I'd convinced myself it was simply some rogue kids up to no good. I wasn't entirely wrong.

The truth was, I had gotten lazy. This life on Earth had taken its toll on me over time, and I needed to step up my game. Indulging was fun, but it seemed this city needed a reminder of who I was and what I was truly capable of.

The idea all of these events were somehow linked wasn't something I hadn't considered, and it was time to crack down again to show the citizens who owned this side of the damn city. Because anyone who fucked with me would pay for it. I didn't spend almost a decade building this shit up only to have it taken from me like that other fucker did, and if the people needed a steady dose of fear and violence to remind them who I was, then so be it.

As I scanned the dance floor and club, it was no surprise to find Cara still watching me. She'd try not to. I could almost see the taut muscles in her neck as she tried desperately to keep her eyes down, but her body betrayed her, and she'd look, and I'd be there, watching her right back. I longed to wrap my fingers around that neck.

Soon, she'd be mine.

I know she could feel the chemistry between us. The electricity that ran through my body when I touched her made her tremble, but her breath would hitch and she'd rub her legs together, desperate for friction against her throbbing clit. She'd look at me sometimes like she thought she understood me. She didn't, no one did. Cara was a confused jumble of naïvety and brash confidence with an I-do-what-I-want attitude thrown on top, and she said she was hiding some darkness within.

I'd spank her bad attitude out of her.

Hearing his footsteps before I saw him when Sven ascended the stairs, I was already snapping my fingers for someone to retrieve my phone that had skidded from the desk onto the floor so I could call the watchman on duty with Ray and Ilsa.

"It happened again, didn't it?"

Sven nodded, and when he opened his mouth to speak, I held my finger up, dialing the phone as it was placed in my open and waiting palm. He answered on the first ring.

"Have they moved? Ray and Ilsa, have they moved?" I barked into the phone.

"No, in fact…" there was a pause and what sounded like laughter, "… I think they know we're watching them.

"Why's that?"

More snickering—they better start taking this shit seriously.

"They're mooning out the window, sir." He chuckled.

"They're fucking *what?*"

"They're pressing their bare asses against the glass. I'm not sure why they think that's a punishment, they are both hot as fu—"

"I know what mooning means, asshole!"

The snickering stopped abruptly. "Yes, sir. Sorry, sir."

Standing, I paced around the balcony, speaking on the phone as much as I was to Sven. "I want all my buildings and clubs guarded. I want to know everyone who goes in and out. If they're not employees, I want them to come to *me,* and *I'll* question them. I want every club, every lab, every entrance and exit watched at all times. I want to know who the fuck is *fucking with me.*"

The final words were screamed into the phone, and he hastily agreed before hanging up, the phone shattering when I hurled it against the wall. Sven didn't flinch when I rounded on him. The DJ had turned the volume up on the music slightly as I had roared down the phone, and the patrons knew better than to ask questions or even look at what was going on.

Everyone knew better, except for *her*.

"Get my men where they're needed," I yelled, then pointing over the balcony I added, "And bring me *that fucking girl.*"

CHAPTER
9

CARA

As he approached me, I glanced at Maddie.

"That's Sven, one of Emrick's top guys. Just do what he says." Her back stiffened, and she looked at the floor. I frowned. What did she think he was going to do to *her?* Turning, I watched Sven approach. He stopped in front of me, and I found myself wishing I was on the other side of the bar with Maddie and not out in the open where he could grab me. Not that I expected him to, but there was something off about Sven, but I could never put my finger on it. I avoided him at all costs, even more than most people avoided Emrick. His shaved head and as much of his skin as I could see beyond the suit was covered in tattoos of varying colors and styles. He looked like a patchwork of different artists and stories, as though anyone he came across with a tattoo gun he'd let have a go at his skin. I never did like face tattoos. Call it judgmental of me, but honestly, he looked like he'd spent most of his life in prison

Judging by Emrick's employees, it was entirely possible.

"Boss wants you upstairs." He grunted at me.

"I'm sorry... what?"

"You heard. Vodka, glasses. Get up there."

I thought he was going to leave, but he simply crossed his arms over his chest and waited. His brow raised when I didn't move, and Maddie began loading up a tray, not meeting my eyes while she worked. As she helped me balance the tray, Maddie threw me a significant look but said nothing. A shiver passed up my spine, and I couldn't tell if it was fear or trepidation. What sort of mood would he be in? Had things not gone well with the man he brought in? Or had they gone *exceedingly* well, and he wanted to celebrate? It took all of my willpower not to visibly tremble as I passed Sven, balancing the metal tray on shaking hands as he turned and followed close behind me.

All my nerves were on fire, and I hated it wasn't only fear. Sure, there was a good measure of that thrown in, but it was also excitement, like I was being invited to some exclusive high-school party and was going to finally get the chance to hang out with the boy I had a crush on. You know the type, the kid with hair that falls in front of his face so he's constantly flicking it to the side with a jerk of his head. Oh, and he's so brooding, deep, and intelligent, he makes you giddy.

Yeah, it was incredibly messed up *that* I was having this reaction to the situation. I wasn't stupid. I'd grown up in this city and knew enough to know Emrick wasn't the sort of man you trusted to get close enough to touch you. But there was electricity between us, and beyond the blackness, I swear there was a softness to his eyes, pain he was stamping down with anger. Anger at what, I didn't know, but it certainly seemed like the world was paying for whoever had wronged him.

Those eyes had been haunting my dreams since he grabbed me in the kitchen when I first started working here.

While I wasn't kidding myself enough to think I was somehow special, I did wonder what he could do with his hands.

When I reached the top of the stairs, Sven pushed the door open, and as he closed and locked it behind me with a click, I spun on my heel, my other hand shooting up to steady the tray.

It was only Emrick and me up here, alone.

Warmth flushed between my legs. *Aww, hell.*

Emrick sat, sunglasses and hoodie on, his chin resting on his fist as he looked out over the balcony. He hadn't even glanced at me as I came onto the balcony area, but when I didn't move from near the door, his head slowly turned toward me, and he sat up straighter as though he hadn't realized I was there.

"Bring the drinks over here."

There was a darkness to his voice that wasn't there when he had wanted to *chat.* He was commanding, curt, and I found myself reacting to it. I was a jumble of nerves, spending every second deciding how I should play this and every moment arguing with myself as to what I should do.

As if I didn't already know what I was going to do.

But part of me was still fighting this attraction, whatever it was.

Shuffling toward him, I placed the tray on the table and stood again. He simply stared at me, and although I couldn't see his dark eyes behind the lenses, I knew he was looking right at me. I could almost feel his gaze drilling into me. Clearing my throat when it clicked what he was waiting for, I opened the expensive vodka, pouring a generous serving from the frosted bottle and handing him the glass.

"Pour yourself one," he said.

His voice was casual again, as though we were friends meeting up for a chat. But it sounded forced, an edge to it, and his fingers drumming on the arm of the chair gave him away.

He was tired of waiting for me.

"I'm working," I managed to whisper.

His stance changed. "And I'm your boss…" before returning to the lighter tone, "… so pour yourself a glass."

My hands were shaking as I did as I was told, and when I placed the bottle back on the tray, he wrapped a hand around mine. My eyes shot to his. He had taken off his glasses, and once again, I was entranced by his gaze. Holding my hand, he walked me around the table and guided me to sit on his lap. I did so, keeping my posture upright and trying to feel as proper as I could, given the position I was in and how my skirt rode up over my thighs.

Sipping at his vodka, he placed his other hand just above my knee.

"Do you know why I asked you here?"

I had a pretty good idea.

"No."

He growled low and deep in his chest, and when I stiffened, his hand gripped my leg for a moment before relaxing again. He leaned until his lips were next to my ear, and I shuddered again as he whispered, "I think you do."

Swallowing heavily, I felt as though my insides were being charged with electricity, every nerve in my body attuned to him and his touch, the skin on my leg burning under his hand. Every second was a fight within, screaming opposing thoughts at me. I dared not look over the balcony, sure I'd see Maddie looking up at me, begging me with her eyes not to do what she knew I was so tempted to do. Emrick had been in my dreams and on my mind, and when I closed my eyes and laid down at night, his dark form was above me. In the dreamscape, I could barely see him, but touching him felt so real, and every day he became clearer in my dreams.

He was *dangerous.*

What should I do?

Or, more pressing, would I be strong enough to even give myself an option? I didn't want to say no. I wanted his hands on my body, him above me. I wanted him.

"Sir—"

"You can call me Emrick."

"Emrick…" I swallowed. This was harder than I thought it would be. When I imagined this situation, I saw myself remembering my plan and boldly proclaiming *no thank you* before turning to leave, and maybe slapping him or hitting him with the tray or the bottle if he refused my exit. But when I was close to him, his scent, those eyes, and that body—I had no willpower left to fight. The power he exuded only made me wonder what he was capable of in the bedroom. He wouldn't be gentle, but I didn't want him to be. I'd been with gentle lovers, and it did nothing for me, and it had been reinforced in my mind what I liked during the orgy with the client from The Palace that one time. That man had infected me, gotten under my skin, and brought out something in me no one to date had been able to replicate.

The prospect Emrick would be able to fill that void both excited and terrified me.

What did he do that made people leave the next day?

What if I couldn't get enough?

His lips parted as though he was going to kiss my neck, and I realized I hadn't finished my sentence.

"I need to get back to work." I tried one last time to convince myself.

"You haven't touched your drink."

With a shaking hand, I brought the glass to my lips, taking a long sip. Emrick didn't take his eyes off my face. When I cleared my throat and licked my lips, I felt his cock twitch under my ass.

Oh my God, he was hard.

His fingers wandered up my leg until he reached my skirt's hem, and although my breathing hitched, and I think I may have whimpered, I didn't object. Emrick slipped his hand under my skirt and between my thighs, and when I shifted my legs so they were slightly open for him, he groaned.

It was all the invitation he needed.

"Get up."

I stood, and he did too. He was no longer touching me but towering over me as he stood so close I could almost feel the rise and fall of his chest with his breathing.

"There's a door behind me. Go."

I did.

Why didn't I even hesitate? I tried not to overthink it.

His commanding me made me want to fall to my knees and please him. The fear of the unknown crawled under my skin and only served to increase my excitement, and while I resented that part of me, at the moment, I was embracing it.

Because there was no fighting this anymore.

Coming into an office, I turned as I heard him follow me before locking the door. His dark eyes were blazing, and I wanted to run my fingers through his hair, to pull the tie out and make him look even wilder. With a flick of his arm, he indicated the elevator door past the desk, and I hastily walked past, scared that if I stopped or slowed down to think, even for a second, I'd lose my nerve.

The elevator went up a single floor, opening to an open-plan apartment.

He waved his arm forward, indicating a room at the end.

The bedroom.

Of course, I knew where this was leading, but the sight of the large room, almost empty except for the king bed against the opposite wall, I twisted my hands together as my nerves got the better of me.

What if I was no good, and he didn't like me?

God, why do I even care what he thinks?

Emrick followed me, again locking the door behind him.

Three locked doors now lay between an exit and me.

He had collected the bottle of vodka from the balcony and was taking a large swig as he shrugged off his hoodie, letting it drop to the floor. He had only a tank underneath it, and the definition of the muscles on his chest and arms were only enhanced by the artistic placement of the tribal tattoos. He looked like a bodybuilder, and it occurred to me I hadn't seen his arms bare before. They were just as intimidating as the rest of him—rock hard and ready to inflict damage.

Oh God. Oh God. Oh God. What was I doing here?

Emrick held the bottle out to me, and when I shook my head rapidly, he waved it slightly. "It'll take the edge off. You're nervous. Drink." His tone was clipped as though he was barely containing anger.

He was barely containing something.

Taking the bottle, I took a swig, longer than I had planned, and despite the purity of the vodka, I still coughed. He chuckled as he took the bottle from me and put it on the floor by his feet before crossing the room and closing the gap between us.

"I may hurt you..." he said. "But I promise you this, you *will* come." Whimpering, I couldn't move, let alone nod. He continued, "This is your last chance to leave. I won't stop you, but if you don't want this, you need to go. *Now.*" His fingers twitched as though he was going to grab me, but he still had some restraint left in him. "Because once I start, I won't stop."

Swallowing heavily, my mind was racing. I wanted a man who could bring out the devil in me, who would dominate and make me orgasm only when he gave his permission. To me, that was so hot. But Emrick, he was a whole new level of darkness, something else entirely, and I didn't know if I was ready for him.

When I took half a step back, his expression darkened, and his lip lifted into a snarl.

But he didn't move.

CHAPTER
10

EMRICK

She was in the bedroom. I had gotten her this far, and *now* she was moving away from me. It was only a half-step, but it was enough. Saying nothing, I watched her. It was written all over her face she was still debating internally. I wouldn't force her. I wanted her screams to be of pleasure, not of terror. If Cara wouldn't let me take her, I would have to go out—right now—and find someone who would.

But I wanted *her*.

She had made me choose her, and she didn't even realize it. The way she kept watching me from the moment she started working here, all that curiosity, fear, and arousal mingled together, I had to have her, her attitude, and her claims of internal darkness. She had intrigued me more, and I simply must take her. She wouldn't come back—they never did. But if one night was all I got with this woman, one night where I could peel back those layers of clothing and confirm what I already suspected—she *wanted* me to be rough—then I'd make it one night worthwhile.

"I'll stay."

After a pause, I growled out, "Say it again."

She was rubbing her upper arm. "I'll stay," she said, so quietly it was little more than a whisper. But when she looked up at me, she straightened her back and jutted out her chest. I was more of a legs and ass man, but she had nice tits. "I'm staying. I want this." This time it was said firmly, and I wondered if she was trying to convince herself or me.

I didn't care.

"Good."

Closing the gap between us again, the back of her legs was right up against the mattress as I kissed her neck. She pouted as though she thought I was going to kiss her, but that wasn't me. Kissing was intimate, kissing was for lovers, and I hadn't kissed anyone in a long time. Cara moaned with my attentions to her neck, and despite the rage running through my veins, the need for release, I knew enough to know I needed to ease her into it. At least at the start. Her body was still slightly stiff against mine, but when I ran my tongue up her neck and over her earlobe, she lifted a leg around my thigh and ran her hands up my back. The heat between her legs was so intense, and I didn't know how long I'd be able to maintain control.

Maybe she didn't want me to.

The way she had been watching me this whole time, it was like she wanted to unleash the beast inside.

She may regret that.

But that wasn't my problem.

Gripping her ass with both hands, I sucked on her neck, definitely leaving a mark and glad of it as I grunted, rutting against her, and she moaned from the feel of the outline of my cock between her legs. She was tiny. I'd enjoy spreading her thighs and making her take every inch. I was holding her up, pressing my erect length against her heat, too many layers of clothing between us.

Spinning her around, I yanked her top down, pinning her arms to her side, and slammed her back against my chest. Holding her close with an arm across her stomach, I brushed the underside of her breasts. Cara moaned as I kissed and nipped my way down her neck, and when I bit into her shoulder, she cried out and struggled against my grip and teeth.

The air was knocked from her lungs when I crushed her against me with both arms, jerking her still with the rough movement. "Shh," I whispered. "I said I might hurt you, but you stayed anyway."

She was whimpering as I traced my lips along her neck before marking her delicate skin with my teeth again.

When she cried out, I spun her around to face me. "I *told* you I might hurt you." She had stopped struggling and was simply staring into my eyes as though searching to find if she could trust me by simply looking hard enough.

You can't trust me, Cara.

I'm not good for humans.

For anyone.

I am one of the fallen.

She was squirming again, and I thought she was trying to break free of my grip on her arms. I growled at her, pressing her harder against me until I realized she was only trying to untangle herself from her top. Kneeling in front of her, I rolled her top down and yanked it over her waist, collecting her skirt in my fingers and peeling that down too. She stepped out of the clothes, and I ran my teeth over her stomach. Cara sucked her stomach in, shrinking away from my touch, but shuddered when I licked over the front of her panties.

She looked good naked. The slight wave of her dark chestnut hair that sat just below her shoulders tempted me. She should grow it out, then I'd have more to grab.

Taking off my boots, I pulled off my tank as I stood. When she went to run her hands up my back,

I slapped her arms away. Cara pouted as if I hurt her feelings and pride more than a physical pain. But she needed to understand we weren't about to make love. I was going to fuck her into tomorrow. Nothing more than a physical release and absolute pleasure for both of us.

Testing the waters, I leaned forward and kissed her neck again, and her skin exploded in goose bumps under my touch. Cara tensed when I dragged my teeth over her skin, and while I clamped down, I didn't bite quite as hard as before and hummed as she sighed with pleasure. Dipping a hand down the front of her panties, she gasped when I ran a finger down her slit.

"You're wet for me." I growled, and she whimpered again, the whimper turning into a moan as I pushed two fingers inside her, groaning at how she stretched around me. Pumping my fingers in, she lifted her leg over my thigh again, and I chuckled. "You want it so bad, don't you?"

"Please..." She was grinding against my palm, and when I bit her neck again, she yelped, her hand shooting up and bunching my hair between desperate fingers. I couldn't tell if she was trying to pull me closer or push me away, and I didn't particularly care. I simply continued to finger fuck her tight little cunt as I kept her still with my jaw. Delicious whimpers and moans fell from her lips as she fidgeted under my touch, and I clamped down harder on her shoulder with my teeth.

If she kept fidgeting like that against me, I might draw blood.

Evidently, she came to the same conclusion and stilled as my thumb found her clit. *Fuck,* she was so wet around my fingers, so tight, it would feel so good to force my cock into her.

But not yet.

Rubbing her clit, I brought her toward her peak, chuckling as she clamped hard around my fingers, desperate to keep me inside her. When Cara began panting, and when I could feel she was on the edge, I withdrew my hand. She clamped her legs together, trying to keep me there, and I laughed quietly again. My amusement angered her, and she started fighting against me, scrambling to clutch onto my shoulders and lifting her hips toward me, wanting my hand back, needing the release I had denied her.

"Not yet, pussycat… only when I say."

"Emrick—"

She yelped when I grabbed a handful of her hair, and her fingers ceased their ministrations along my shoulders. I didn't want her to touch my scars. I didn't want her pity or her questions. She wasn't to touch me without permission. Her eyes found mine, and we stared hard at each other, her head tilted to the side with my grip on her hair.

Grunting, I yanked down her underwear and, with a hand on her shoulder, pushed her to her knees, keeping my fingers twisted in her hair. She was already undoing my pants before I said anything, and I snatched her wrists together, holding them above her head.

"You only touch me when I say, you only move when I say, and you only come when *I say.* Do you understand?"

"Yes."

"Put your hands behind your back and keep them there, or I'll *tie* them there."

She nodded and parted her lips, making me chuckle again. Apparently, she wasn't nervous anymore, practically begging for my cock. I undid and dropped my pants, kicking them to the side and rubbing my erect length in front of her face, watching her eyes watch me.

"Open your mouth," I said, and she did without hesitation. "Wider." Grabbing her neck, I leaned down, loving how her eyes widened when my fingers gripped her throat. "I said, fucking *wider.*"

She whimpered against my grip, and I tightened it, feeling her throat move under my palm. Her shoulders shook, but she didn't move her hands from behind her back and opened her mouth wide like a good little whore.

"Good girl."

This wasn't the time for *slowly,* and I didn't know if I'd be able to contain myself even if she were expecting that sort of treatment. She was as responsive as I'd known she'd be, and when I held her head still and slid my cock into her waiting mouth, she groaned around my length, sending vibrations through me.

"Keep that mouth open, pussycat," I muttered, and winding my fingers through her hair, I began to fuck her mouth. It was messy, she was drooling, but she kept her tongue out and mouth open like a fucking good girl. When I pressed in deep and held my cock there, she whimpered against me, her nose buried in my pubic hair. Pulling her back, she gasped, and I was impressed she had kept her hands behind her back and not gripped my thighs or tried to push me away.

Cara's eyes flashed with lust, and a low growl rumbled through my throat.

She fucking loves it.

When I did it again, she held my eye contact, even as her eyes started to water. This wasn't bringing me close as I wasn't moving, but it wasn't about that. The power of holding her there, knowing she was submitting entirely to me, knowing I was in charge of when she breathed freely next, sent electricity pulsing through me. I couldn't keep from growling as I fucked her mouth, loud and animalistic as I took her.

Fuck.

Unable to wait longer, I pulled her to her feet, steadying her when she stumbled slightly from the roughness and speed of being pulled upright. Cara giggled when she fell back against me, and that turned into another squeal when I wound my fingers around her throat, slamming her back against my chest and grinding my erect length against her ass.

"You love it, don't you?" I whispered in her ear, and when she simply moaned but didn't answer, I sunk my teeth into her neck again. She was going to be marked tomorrow. "Tell me you love it."

"I love it, sir."

A shudder ran down my spine at her tone, heavy with lust and arousal. I hadn't told her to call me *sir*, but she had done it anyway. Fuck, she was something else. "Get on the fucking bed. Bend over."

Letting her throat go, I shoved her forward, and she stumbled before obeying my command, presenting me with her perfectly curved ass and pussy, dripping wet and waiting for me. Cara moaned deep and long as I penetrated her in one smooth motion. She was gripping me so perfectly, I grabbed her shoulders as I pushed through the final bit of resistance until I was fully sheathed within her.

"You're going to come for me," I muttered as I wrapped an arm around her, finding her clit with my fingers and rubbing it in small, tight circles. "You're going to come around my cock."

"Yes..." she whispered, grinding her hips against me as I rubbed her clit, thrusting slow and deep into her and coating my cock in her juices.

She was already so close, and her squeaks and cries as she neared her peak were ecstasy. I needed her to come, to tighten around me so I could destroy her in chase of my own high. It was never enough, each orgasm only driving me toward the next. These were forbidden delights, earthly pleasures which angels weren't supposed to partake in.

But I had broken the ultimate rule and cared about none of the others now.

She was mine to use and enjoy.

By the time she came, I was already thrusting hard into her, her pussy tightening as I jerked within her, forcing her to open as she clamped around me. When she sighed with satisfaction, I withdrew my hand and gripped her hips, angling her ass so she was completely at my mercy and I could get in deep.

When I began thrusting harder, she cried out each time I was completely inside her, but I no longer cared about her comfort, although the way her cunt flushed with warmth with every thrust told me comfort wasn't an issue for the little whore. I focused only on the feeling building within me, that taste of heaven I could only reach through the act of carnal desires. Why God would hide this level of pleasure in an act we were not supposed to do, in an act most humans still felt taboo, ashamed of their own desires and passions, I wasn't sure. Some sick irony, perhaps. But between her legs was heaven, and as she twitched, pushing back to me when I thought she'd try to move away, my fingers dug into her hips.

"Emrick!" she cried out as I leaned forward, hitting a new spot and creating a new sensation within her, and her moans jerked off into screams when I sunk my teeth into her shoulder, holding her still while I fucked her. Her skin was so delicate, so fragile, and I loved the feel of it in my mouth and between my teeth. She lifted a hand then in what I'm sure was an attempt to fight me off, but when she found my thigh and gripped it with her nails, the pain only added to my pleasure.

"Let me," I mumbled against her skin as I dragged my teeth across her back. "*Let me.*"

She cried out again when I bit into her other shoulder, and I mumbled *fuck* against her skin as she clamped around me. I was close, so close to that moment I chased, the drawn-out pleasure almost made me forget my anger and centered me completely.

With a loud groan, I came inside her, my teeth cutting into her as I continued pumping for a few more strokes before pulling out. Cara collapsed on the bed, her back dotted with blood from my teeth, and her pussy dripping with our cum. She was whimpering slightly, her leg twitching intermittently.

Sitting on the edge of the bed, I ran my fingers through my hair.

I'd be ready to go again soon.

But first.

Cara moaned when I leaned across the bed, grabbed her legs, and dragged her toward me.

"Come now, pussycat... you didn't think we'd be done so soon?"

"Emrick..." she whispered, trailing off into nothing as I pulled her stomach down over my lap.

"Tell me."

"I came so hard," Cara muttered, burying her face into the bed sheets and groaning, her body limp and at my whim.

"And you'll come again."

"Oh God..."

"God's not here, only me." She shuddered as I caressed her ass, and when she was practically purring, I landed a hard slap on her cheek. She cried out, and on reflex, tried to lift herself from me. With another slap, she laid back down, accepting her punishment.

"I'm going to spank you, pussycat."

Slap.

"Until your ass is a pretty shade of pink."

Slap.

"Then I'm going to fuck you again."

Slap.

"Okay?"

"Yes, s—" She jumped as I slapped her again before I paused to admire the hue her skin was taking on. Gripping around her hips, I lifted her and leaned in to run my tongue between her ass cheeks, causing her to squeal again. She was mine tonight to do with what I pleased, to use as I wanted until I was too exhausted to go on. She'd run out of energy long before I did, and if she simply wanted to lay there while I fucked her one final time, that was fine with me.

Another slap.

Another squeal of pleasure mingled with pain.

And so much more to come.

CHAPTER
11

CARA

The sunlight streaming insistently through the far window woke me, and I was initially surprised to find I had woken before Emrick. Although perhaps I shouldn't be, we went for hours last night, and I was completely exhausted at the end, collapsing and falling asleep almost immediately when he pulled his cock from my mouth after coming for what I think was the fifth time. Maybe the seventh, I had no idea. I probably came almost twice as many times, and again when I didn't think I had anything more to give, he'd draw another orgasm from me with his fingers. I'd never known a man to have that kind of stamina—Emrick overrode the memory of the client from The Palace.

I had the marks to show for it, and short of wearing a turtleneck to work, there'd be no way to cover the bruises on my neck and teeth marks on my back and shoulders. No one would see the red of my ass, though, thankfully, although I'm sure I'd feel it for a few days when I sat down.

Whatever, I'll wear the marks with pride.

He was incredible. His touch was rough, and he'd push me to the edge of my limits, but not beyond. Was it intentional? I couldn't be sure. There wasn't much about Emrick I'd describe as gentle, but when I thought I couldn't take any more, he would reward me with an earth-shattering orgasm, it was worth it.

I could see how that treatment might scare some people away, and what did it say about me since I was still here? That all I could think about was wanting *more?* Shrugging to myself, I stretched my legs out under the sheet. I already knew I was messed up inside, so this wasn't news to me.

Rolling over, I watched him breathe. He had his back turned to me, and frowning, I gently pulled the light sheet off him, slapping a hand to my mouth to contain my gasp.

Never have I seen scars like that before.

Large crescent moon-shaped scars trailing from his shoulders almost down to his hips. Two shapes curving toward each other, his skin looking as though it had been burned or branded, thick scar tissue of twisted pinks and whites filled the moon shapes, the skin stretched and blotchy.

Whatever caused those scars must have been incredibly painful, and I wondered if they had something to do with his rage at the world and everyone within it. He was always so angry, and I assumed it was a defense mechanism for dealing with this business. But now I wasn't so sure. Someone had hurt him incredibly badly, and maybe all of this was him seeking revenge on the world when he couldn't get to the one who had caused the pain.

Maybe I was hoping to see something inside him that wasn't there.

Biting my bottom lip, I reached out my hand, brushing my fingers gently across the scars' surface. I screamed when, in one smooth motion, Emrick rolled over and snatched my hand from the air before pouncing on me, pinning me down with my hands on either side of my head. His dark eyes flashed with rage, and he was breathing like a wounded bull. He'd gone from peaceful slumber to an animal in seconds.

"I... I'm sorry," I whispered. "I didn't mean—"

"*Don't ever.* Don't touch. Not *ever*. Don't."

His words were broken up, barely distinguishable through the anger battling within him. His grip on my wrists was painful, but I didn't move. He was feral at that moment, and I searched his eyes for a glimpse of the Emrick I had seen last night—the Emrick who had come out of his shell to play, who had unleashed his desires on me, and who looked almost happy at times, his eyes lighting up when I came at his touch.

Where had that man gone?

My eyes darted between his as his breathing slowed, but he continued to glare at me. His hair falling wild around his face, he looked almost unhinged. I had pushed some boundary, that much was abundantly clear.

"I'm sorry," I whispered. Unsure what else to say.

With a heavy grunt, his breathing returned to normal, and the frown melted from his face, returning to the same stoic expression he usually held. After a pause, he said, "You're still here."

Panic filled me again, and I glanced at his grip on my hands.

How many ways could I screw this up? *Was I supposed to leave?*

I'd taken a hell of a chance coming to bed with him, knowing it was against not only my better judgment but the advice of almost everyone in the club. Was this what happened to everyone else? Were they fired because they couldn't take the hint and get out of his room after fucking?

"I'm sorry." I felt like I was apologizing a lot, but what else could I do? "I didn't know I was supposed to leave."

His eyes searched mine, his grip on my wrists slackening slightly, but he didn't let me up. I flexed my hands, and his gaze flickered to the movement. It was becoming increasingly difficult not to feel exposed under his glare. Despite everything last night, he hadn't looked at me like this, like he was trying to read my mind or figure me out. I wanted to tell him there was nothing to figure out, I was—mostly—an open book. What you see is what you get.

"Why don't you tattoo over the scars?"

His expression went dark. "What?"

It was hard to keep my voice bold under the way he was staring at me. *If looks could kill.* "If you hate them so much, why don't you tattoo over them?"

"I can't."

"Why?"

Those eyes were so dark, and I was lost in the black of him and his gaze. "You ask a lot of questions."

"I'm curious about you."

"You apparently know everything about me, everyone does. I'm sure you've heard it all."

"I want to hear it from you."

And it was true. While I knew the rumors were most likely true, and chances are he had done things even worse than what people whispered about, things no one knew of or dared to speak. I wanted to know the man behind those eyes, the man behind the darkness that ebbs and flows around him.

The man who had suffered and ended up with those scars.

But Emrick simply stared at me before asking, "Did I hurt you last night?"

"Yes." I squirmed again, not so much from being pinned underneath his body but from the way he was looking at me, studying me. Feeling my face flush, I hated it, but there was nothing I could do to hide it. My voice was small when I added, "But I liked it."

Why was it so hard to admit? I guess it was merely another part of my darkness I hadn't owned up to yet.

"I bit you. I spanked you..." He paused, glancing at my neck, where I'm sure the bruises were starting to show. "I drew blood."

I held his stare. "I know. I was there."

Emrick frowned, staring at me hard. *What did he want from me?*

He released my hands with a push against the pillows, and I stayed with my arms up as he traced his fingers down and over my breasts, flicking his thumbs over my nipples.

"What are you doing?" I whispered.

I squealed as he pinched my nipples, and he continued to stare into my eyes. "What do you think I'm doing?"

"I thought you wanted me to leave."

His lips twitched—it was almost a smile. "I

thought so too. But now I want to play with my toy again." He slapped my hand away when I went to touch his hair. "Keep your hands above your head, pussycat."

My skin tingled as he glided his hands down my body, and when I felt his breath against my mound, I trembled. Emrick looked up at me. God, he was so damn hot. Those eyes drove me wild—black like the night sky, a world of danger hidden there. Like this—with his hair out of the ponytail he usually kept it in and strands of dark hair falling across his face—he looked like the devil himself.

With his hands splayed across my stomach and thighs, I felt small and vulnerable. Added to that there was very real danger he could hurt me, and I couldn't be sure what he was thinking at any given moment and what he would do to me. He was an enigma.

I didn't think he would hurt me, not really, not beyond the mixture of pleasure and pain he had already exposed me to.

Or was that just a taste of what he was capable of?

But I know I was basing my faith he wouldn't hurt or kill me on almost nothing. What did I know about this man, really? Rumors and snippets, glances and shared looks, meaningless chatting and a night of absolute pleasure, and nothing much beyond. He could be anybody, and then with how he looked at me when I had stayed the night, like I was as much a mystery to him as he was to me.

I groaned and gripped the pillow when he flicked his tongue between my pussy lips and over my clit. He never took his eyes off me. Every time I looked down, he was watching me, taking in every jerk, twitch, and cry as he sucked on my clit. I wasn't going to last long if he kept doing that.

Emrick roughly spread my legs, breathing my scent in, sending another shiver down my spine. His mouth moved to me, and I closed my eyes a moment after he did before he pushed his tongue inside me. I was writhing under his touch, about to lose my control and grip of his hair, desperate to pull him toward me, when he moved away—a harsh and violent motion.

"Emrick," I whispered, still grinding my hips against a touch that was no longer there.

"Get out."

I stuttered, "W-what?"

The moment was shattered as he kneeled between my legs, his eyes blazing with fury that had me shrinking away from him, covering my chest with my hands. He pointed to the door, bellowing, "Get the fuck out! Get out! *Get out!*"

I've never moved so fast in my life. He radiated danger, his breathing ragged as he balled his hands into shaking fists by his side. I bounded off the bed, throwing confused glances at him while I dressed.

His mouth was still glistening with my juices. He noticed me looking and wiped his lips with the back of his hand before spitting on the bed where I had been.

When I didn't move fast enough, he came barreling toward me, and I hurried to finish dressing, still pulling the straps of my top over my shoulders as he fumbled with the lock on the bedroom door and shoved me out into the main room.

"Emrick—"

But he had slammed the bedroom door in my face. Turning, I paused, unsure what to do. It seemed foolish to hang around or try to see him again, so I walked to the elevator and took it down to the office. When the doors slid open, the office wasn't empty. Sven and another of Emrick's men were seated around, their quiet chatting ceasing when they looked at me. My face flushed when they smirked, and Sven sauntered to the balcony door to unlock it, chuckling, laughing *at* me. I was a joke to them. Keeping my head down, I rushed past them, barely keeping the tears at bay as I threw the final door open and ran down the stairs.

What the hell happened?

A scolding hot shower.

But it wasn't enough.

I knew what last night was—sex for pleasure and nothing more. Yet somehow, I had come away feeling more used than I ever had before, and I'd been with some terrible men. This morning had cemented my resolve to leave. I'd done exactly what I told myself I wouldn't, and for some reason, convinced myself there was more to Emrick than stories and what meets the eye. But he was just as bad as everyone said he was. I could take a one-night stand, but the way he had looked at me as though I were scum, barely allowing me the time to dress before physically pushing me out the door made me sick.

The rage in his eyes, that was something else entirely, and I had no idea what I'd done to bring it on.

The small wounds dotted on my body throbbed—in hindsight, the piping hot water may not have been a good idea, all it did was increase blood flow and make my bruises feel worse than they actually were.

The hot water blasted against my body, and after

half an hour, the confusion and frustration were making way for something else. Something stirred inside me, born from the pit of darkness and living behind the façade I displayed. I ignored it because I knew what happened when I felt like that, and I couldn't trust myself any more than I could trust anyone else. After *the incident,* the day that messed me up and awakened the dark part of me which thrived in the chaos, I had tried to keep this particular feeling to a minimum.

The feeling in the pit of my stomach, I tried to convince myself it was self-pity, but after a drink and collapsing in bed, I admitted what it was.

Rage.

Because who the hell was he to treat me like that? Emrick was the one who had wanted *me* to come to *him*. All I did was watch him, and I could have hardly been the first who did that. He draws the eye with his striking good looks and the dark aura which follows him around. Emrick came to me on more than one occasion and asked me to come to his room. I tried, God knows I tried to resist him. So when I finally did give in, he treats me like *that?* Screw that for a joke.

He may be accustomed to treating people like garbage, but that doesn't mean I have to throw away my job as well because he threw a fit.

If he were expecting me not to be at work tonight, he was in for a shock.

After a few hours of much-needed sleep, I was back at Urban, doing my best to ignore the stares from patrons and bouncers alike at the smattering of injuries across my skin. The bruises had only gotten worse over the past few hours, and my neck and shoulders looked like I'd done three rounds in a boxing ring. But screw it. Up until Emrick's tantrum, I'd had a great night, and there was no shame in that.

Maddie wasn't in tonight. I thought she was rostered, but maybe I was mistaken, or maybe she was sick, but usually, she'd text me about something like that. I was thankful, though, and not in the mood to deal with her judgment about giving into the temptation that existed in the form of the boss of this club, not to mention the boss of half the underground crime in the city. But perhaps Maddie didn't understand me as well as she thought she did. Few people knew the truth of my past—that was between me, the police, and my ex-boyfriend.

And the victims, who could no longer tell their side.

Emrick had been a hell of a temptation, but he'd left a bad taste in my mouth, and rather than aching for him physically, I was aching to wrap my fingers around his throat. A flicker of a grin passed over my face at the thought. I knew violence should be avoided at all costs. Violence came with a heavy price, but sometimes it solved the problem too.

Sometimes violence was all they understood.

The night was uneventful, and something about that left me feeling empty. I was ready for a confrontation, ready to give someone a piece of my mind in lieu of Emrick, but I hadn't even seen him on the balcony tonight.

Toward the end of my shift, I was heading back to the bar with an empty tray, and yelped involuntarily as I was yanked sideways into a small hall which led to the bathrooms.

The tray clanged to the floor, and then Emrick was behind me. I didn't need to ask who it was to know it was him. I was familiar enough with the feeling of my back against his hard chest, his arms wrapped around my body, and his breath against my neck. He had one arm wrapped around my stomach and the other forearm pressing between my breasts as he gripped my throat, his large hand encompassing my neck and fingers wrapping around, threatening me with their size alone. My neck ached where his fingers pressed against the bruises, but I felt a flush between my legs at his proximity.

He smelled so good.

Emrick's chest rose and fell against me with his breathing—heavy, deep, almost labored breaths.

He was angry.

That made two of us.

"What are you doing here?" he hissed.

Twisting my neck until he slightly loosened his grip, I gasped a breath, trying to glare at him out of the corner of my eye before answering, "I work here."

"Don't give me cheek, you little bitch. I mean, why did you come back?" His breath was hot against my neck as he snarled the words into my ear, keeping quiet even though it was unnecessary over the pounding music.

"I told you, I work here. Or was your little fit this morning supposed to be you firing me?" His fingers tightened around my neck at my comment, and when I tried to twist away from him, he crushed me against him. The breath was knocked from me when his back hit the wall and he held me to him, absorbing the impact together. Clutching at his forearm, I gripped with my nails into his skin, warning him without words. Emrick simply continued to heave angry breaths against me, so I dug my nails into his arm until I drew blood. Only then did he loosen his grip. But it was after a pause, and if I didn't know better, it almost sounded like he chuckled.

"You're such a fucking slut. You'll fuck anyone,

won't you?"

He was practically spitting the words out, hate dripping from every syllable.

Where the hell was all this coming from?

"I sleep with who I want to, *sir.*" This time there was a definite chuckle, but there was no humor behind it, and I'd have smiled coldly if I wasn't so pissed off. What was he playing at? I couldn't wrap my head around his actions, seeming to change and switch with the wind and his whims. "I bet you treat all the girls like this." I sneered at him.

He spun me around then, and on reflex, I lifted my arms between us, forced to slam my forearms against his chest as he yanked me against him. He tilted his head down and assessed me over the top of his sunglasses, holding me still with those dark eyes. Almost black, like his soul.

And mine.

"Not all the girls," he whispered. "Only you."

He was so close, and I watched his lips. There was no smile or hint of humor, only pressed into a thin line as his anger pulsed from him. I couldn't figure out what it was I had done to enrage him so, but if he weren't man enough to tell me, then I wasn't going to feel bad about it. I owed him nothing but a night's work for the pay I earned, and that's all.

Emrick moved closer, and I gasped when I thought he was going to kiss me. But he stopped, moments from contact, so close I could almost feel the brush of his lips against mine.

I wanted him and found myself slightly pouting my lips.

So close.

In a second, his demeanor changed, and he thrust me hard away from him, and I fell against the opposite wall as he muttered, "Get back to work, slut," before disappearing around the corner and back into the club.

Staring after him, I rubbed my arms, a chill over me now his warmth wasn't near.

What the hell was that about?

I was still no closer to an answer.

CHAPTER 12

EMRICK

That fucking slut, I don't know why I was expecting anything different from her.

Everyone else left after a night with me, every single one of them, as though they were afraid I'd take it further and kill them if they came back. They'd disappear out the back with their bruises and bite marks, proverbial tail between their legs, and slink down the alley, never to be seen again. Killing them would serve no purpose, and I didn't get off on murder. Killing was only to be used when it was absolutely necessary, and given I had been dumped on Earth and pushed into a corner where I had to do what I needed to, it was necessary more than I perhaps would have liked. I didn't enjoy it, not since the first time.

Not my fault.

This is the point I had tried to get across to my brothers and sisters—and Cara was a perfect example of it—that demons did whatever the hell they wanted without thought for the consequences. Oh, they claimed they cared about the rules, but why was it right they could, on occasion, tear people apart and if not kill them, then practically leave them for dead, and yet when I did the same, I fell?

No amount of explanation made it right. I was told it wasn't my call to decide who lived or died. But if the higher power controlled all, if we were all just pawns in his game, then humans coming across my path who died at my hand were fated to do so, right?

Wrong, apparently. I was a servant to God, and I should know better. I could not be manipulated like demons and could not be used—all my will was my own.

Or so I was told.

Yet He let the demons roam the Earth, allowed them to do as they pleased—rise through the ranks, become powerful among humans, claim humans as their mates, and partake in earthly pleasures.

But angels, no, that life wasn't for us. We were held to a higher calling.

I had done what I did without mercy and regret. So now, I was taking my part of this world, claiming this city and making it my own.

By any means necessary.

And fucking demons just took whatever they goddamn wanted.

Cara tasted like him. It didn't matter how long ago it was. It didn't matter she didn't know me then. She was marked by him.

A fucking *demon.*

She'd fucked a goddamn demon, more than once, in some sort of vile demon-human orgy. Whether she knew his true nature was irrelevant, Cara had allowed herself to be used by a minion of Hell and was tainted beyond repair. No wonder she responded so vigorously to my rough treatment. She *loved* it, she *craved* it. After being with *him,* nothing less would do to get her off.

For a moment, I thought she was different. Fuck knows why, but she was this strange combination of fear and anger, of darkness and light. Spitting out retorts like she wasn't afraid, then trembling when I got too close to her. Oh, I had longed to pull her layers away and learn what made her tick. I wanted to find out who she was beyond fucking her, something I hadn't considered for years.

But no. It could never be. There would never be another.

I didn't have it in me anymore. There was nothing left of the Emrick from all those years ago, not after all the things I had done.

Grinding out a groan between clenched teeth,

the glass in my hand shattered. Tate raised his head from his drink, casting a sideways glance at me.

"Boss?" he muttered. There wasn't concern in his tone, and he sounded almost disinterested. I imagined he was inquiring out of duty more than anything.

That was fine with me as that was all the connection I wanted and deserved anymore.

"I fucking hate demons, you know that?" I spat out. Tate pulled a face, and as I tugged the pieces of glass from my hand and flicked them into an ashtray, I scoffed at him. "Oh, fuck off with that look, Tate, you're not even a real demon."

He looked like he was about to hit me, but he wouldn't dare, not with the bodyguards around. Sometimes I suspected he wanted to deck me, and one day he'd catch me in the wrong mood, and I might take him up on that. It made no difference to me he didn't like how I ran my business sometimes. If he hated it so much, he could fuck off. Demons, or even humans with demon blood, were useful because of their strength and stamina. Tate had been loyal and helpful, but no one was irreplaceable.

Almost no one.

"Any word?" I snapped at him, pulling my sleeve down and clenching my fist over the fabric to stop the bleeding. Tate stared at me for a moment longer before answering, holding on to whatever level of power he thought he had within this building.

"They got the guys. They're bringing them in."

"Good."

There had been another fire, this time at one of my largest clubs—other than this one—Spicy. I fucking hated the name, but the signage was already there from the previous owner, and it seemed a waste to rebrand it when all I was really interested in was the basement. That large area immediately under the feet of drunken clubgoers served as the perfect space for our specialized *chefs* to work, and the club itself to be used for distribution. Hell, all our main clientele was right there—I never even had to consider shipping to other cities. This hellhole snorted and swallowed all the merchandise I could produce.

Problem was, there weren't many people who knew Spicy was one of *mine*, and I liked to keep it that way. So, either it was a massive coincidence they had hit that club as well as my other buildings, or—a much more sinister and unfortunately more likely scenario—they knew *exactly* what they were doing and had somehow gotten information few people had.

Earlier, my gaze had scanned the club floor, and I had scowled when I saw Cara and I turned away before she could look at me. Because she *would* look at me, she always did. Forcing my thoughts back to the job at hand, I thought, *who in this club was betraying me?*

Inside or outside job, either way, I was about to find out. I supposed it was only a matter of time before someone turned on me.

This time the culprits hadn't succeeded in completely burning down the place, and I hadn't lost any of my merchandise. Lucky for them. The guilty were incredibly clever about it, as though they knew the situation had changed, and my places were being watched now. Rather than sneaking in after hours and destroying an almost empty building or waiting until it was final call to minimize the potential collateral damage as they had previously, they came in during one of the busiest hours and tried to start a fire while the place was packed.

Either they stopped caring about people getting hurt or killed, or they were holding on to some naïve hope the place would be evacuated before any irreversible damage was done.

Definitely not Ray's work—she wouldn't take the risk.

They would have gotten away with the attempt if it weren't for one of my men about to take a piss at that moment. While sometimes it helped when things played out in my favor, I didn't like leaving things to coincidence. It made me feel like *someone* was interfering where they shouldn't.

Two men and a woman were dragged up the

stairs, across the balcony, and deposited at my feet as I sat in my office. This time, I'd had Tate lay out plastic ahead of time, and despite trying to hide it, they were already terrified before I'd even done anything to them. Being on a floor covered in plastic surrounded by men like me had that effect on people.

Good.

The woman went to stand, and one of my men kicked her legs out from underneath her. She collapsed before wincing and kneeling next to her comrades.

"You'll stay on your knees," Tate hissed out.

"Who are they?" I asked, looking at the people but directing the question at Sven.

"Patricia, Buddy, Damien. Low-life thugs, shit-for-hire types, too stupid to run something like this themselves."

"Fuck you," Damien spat, earning himself an elbow to the back of the head.

Watching them, my fingers drummed on my cheek. Do I kill them? Seemed pointless at this stage unless they forced my hand. First, I needed to know what they knew.

"Who do you work for?" I asked.

Patricia smirked, her long dirty hair falling around her face. "No one."

"Do I really have to hurt you to get answers?"

Her eyes widened but only for a moment before

the smug look returned. It was a façade, the fear was heavy in her eyes, and she wasn't the only one. Damien might have had the balls to back chat my guys, but Buddy hadn't said a word. His jaw was clenched tight, and eyes were darting around the room, no doubt looking for an escape.

He was the weak link.

With a tilt of my head in his direction, Buddy was grabbed and dragged across the floor until he was at my feet, practically between my legs. I leaned forward in my chair and wrapped my hands around his throat.

Not too tight, just a warning.

For now.

"Who do you work for?"

"N-no one."

But his tone wasn't as assured as Patricia's, and he wouldn't be able to keep up the lie. Snitches always exposed themselves. Whatever their motivation was for targeting my empire, I doubted Buddy believed in it enough to put his own life on the line.

Smart man.

Tightening my grip, his hands shot to mine, clawing at my fingers as he became more desperate for oxygen. I asked the question again, although I knew he wouldn't be able to answer with the pressure I was applying to his throat. Behind my glasses, my eyes were blazing. I'd use it when the time was right—the black of my eyes always unsettled humans. The sunglasses were to maintain a front, to keep neutral, but also a tool to reveal my true dark nature when I wanted.

Dramatic, maybe, but it worked.

It also meant I could watch my club without anyone being sure exactly where I was looking. It kept people on edge.

"Fuck, man, he can't breathe!" Damien finally spoke up as the color of Buddy's face started to change, bluing as the oxygen failed to reach his brain and his body desperately sought what it could, his skin rapidly shifting between colors. Without loosening my grip, I turned my gaze to Damien.

"That's the point."

"Let him go!"

This plead was from Patricia, and I tilted my head at her before releasing Buddy from my grip. He fell back, scrambling to get away from me as he coughed and spluttered, gasping for air that never felt so precious.

Sliding back in the leather seat, I asked again, "Who do you work for?"

"We don't know," Buddy spluttered.

With a well-aimed kick, I broke his nose, and he was knocked out, falling back with his knees tucked under him. Patricia looked at me with a mixture of rage and fear. "He was telling the truth."

"Yeah? Maybe you just need to jog your memory." When I stood, they cowered but didn't stand to meet me. At least they were good at following orders.

But I already knew that about them.

Someone organized this and knew my largest and most profitable venues. These people were simply pawns, and while once up on a time I would've held a certain level of sympathy for them, my patience was nonexistent at this point. I needed everything they knew to track down whoever was responsible and make them pay.

Remove them from my path, and I could continue to grow my empire.

Make an example of them, so anyone else considering it would think twice.

How much was their life worth?

Grabbing a handful of Patricia's hair, I lifted her to her feet. Damien was on his feet straight away, and I didn't need to know the ins and outs of their relationship to see his protectiveness over her. Humans were so easy to read—Buddy was like the little brother surrogate, but Patricia and Damien, something else was going on there. With those sideways glances they cast each other, those knowing smirks as if to say *we got this, babe.*

We'll see.

Twisting my fist into her hair, I landed a punch against her nose. Damien screamed in rage but could do nothing as Sven wrapped his arms around him, pressing his palms to the top of Damien's head so he was held like some sort of puppet with his arms in the air. Patricia blinked blearily through the droplets of blood splattered over her eyes as she barely held onto consciousness.

"Tell me what you know…" I growled, sliding my glasses off and letting my eyes travel to Damien before finishing my thought, "… or I'll fuck her in front of you, choking her so she takes her last breath when I fill her with cum."

"You sick *fuck!*" Damien cried, while Patricia just groaned, sliding in and out of consciousness.

"Who do you work for?" I bellowed at Damien, and he shrunk away from me, his eyes glazed with rage and fear, flickering between mine and Patricia as she struggled to remain standing.

"We don't know!" he cried back. "Please, it's the truth. I swear, we don't know. Just let her go."

Releasing Patricia's hair, she slumped to her knees, and Damien rushed her as Sven let him go, letting her lean against his legs and brushing her hair with his fingers, whispering sweet nothings and lies about how it was all going to be okay.

Nothing would be okay for them, not now they were on my radar. If they wanted to stop looking over their shoulders, they would need to leave my city.

After they told me what they knew.

And *if* I let them live.

"Tell me what you *do* know," I said, my fingers clenching and releasing at my sides.

There was a shadow of a smirk on Damien's face, and I'm sure if I hadn't threatened Patricia the way I did, he'd be openly laughing in my face.

He *knew* something.

When my arm twitched toward him, he flinched. "It was one of your people."

Silence.

Damien was glancing around the room, but no one but me was looking at him.

All eyes were on me.

"What did you say?"

There was that hint of a smirk again. Was this a fucking game to him?

"You've got a traitor within your mix," Damien said. "Someone is trying to bring you down from the inside." He laughed then, a single loud sound edging with fear and panic. "You're losing your hold on this city, and everyone knows it. People are doing things they wouldn't have *dared* two years ago."

I thought of the people selling products from other providers within my clubs. He was right, no one in their right mind would have dared that before. I was being sabotaged.

Pushing my sunglasses back toward my face with my forefinger, I was able to keep my expression passive as I studied Damien. I was well aware every one of my men was watching me, wondering, *was it true?* Was there really someone within my ranks who was trying to bring me down? Trying to shatter the stranglehold I had on this city? And if so, who and why?

The *why* wouldn't be hard to guess—power bred jealousy, and people wanted what I had.

The *who* might be harder to crack.

My suspicions were confirmed about the origin of their information about Spicy. I kept my groan of impatience deep inside me. God, I hated being right all the fucking time.

My men were losing faith in me and my abilities, and the seconds ticked by in silence while I watched the people on the floor in front of me. Every second I didn't act was making the seed of doubt within them flourish until they wondered if I could even hold my own anymore.

Was I losing my touch?

If these beings were demons, I wouldn't hesitate to kill them.

If I let them live, it would be a sign of weakness.

There was nothing I could do to them that would shock the men in this room, they had seen it all, whether here or in their lives prior to meeting me. They've all witnessed some seriously fucked-up shit. I needed to make an example but keep them guessing, keep them afraid of me.

I needed a plan.

Patricia's eyes had cleared slightly, and she was staring at me with all the others.

I had to act.

"Tie them up, throw them in the back of the van."

Anything left of the smirk dropped from Damien's face. "Wait!"

"I'll take care of them off-site." I was pleased when there was a muffled guffaw from one of the men, his imagination running wild at what punishment I might dish out. My lips twitched. "I know exactly what to do."

CHAPTER
13

CARA

There was an explosion of sound from the back of the club and the hall that led toward the rear exit. The sort of sound most people knew better than to investigate and tried their best to ignore—even though the patrons' strained expressions gave them away. Fighting, screaming, muffled yells, and the sounds of people being dragged echoed their way through the club, barely audible over the music but loud enough I could see the cringe of the shoulders of those closest as they turned their backs, knowing better than to get involved.

Those sounds alone were enough to remind everyone who Emrick was and what he was capable of. Whatever was happening, someone had done something to upset him. All I could think of was the night we had actually spoken on the balcony, the conflict clear on his face even though I couldn't see his eyes when I alluded to my past.

Emrick had been playing some messed-up back-and-forth game with me, and it had to end. All these conflicting thoughts in my head were driving me insane. Maybe if I *saw* it with my own eyes, I could finally slap some sense into myself about what kind of man Emrick really was.

Exactly the stuff I was trying to run away from.

I had to know because there was the lingering doubt within me that my earlier suspicions about something lighter living inside him were true and not simply wishful thinking. We all hoped we could change people, that all the dark and brooding types needed was someone to bring out the best in them. Emrick was far beyond saving, every remaining sane part of me screamed to remind my mind and soul who he was. But once upon a time, I thought *I* had been beyond saving, so there was one tiny fiber, one minuscule bit of doubt telling me *maybe*.

Maybe I could save him, bring him with me, and we could start a new life together.

Maybe we could save each other.

After all, we all had our secrets.

I was laying it all on the line, but there was every chance I'd catch him at the wrong moment, and he'd turn on me. Hell, I had done some stupid things before, and this might be a close second to the most reckless. But I was stubborn, and I simply had to see, to *know*, then maybe I would learn something this time.

Placing the empty tray on the bar, I turned toward the ruckus when Maddie grabbed my arm. "What do you think you're doing?" she hissed at me.

"I just want to see what's going on."

"Are you *out of your mind?*"

Yanking my arm from her grasp, she stared at me, jaw agape. "If you think he's so bad, why do you work for him?"

Maddie stared at me. "The same reason you do… *money*. That's all it comes down to… money! You know that!"

"I'm going," I said, sidestepping another of her attempts to grab me and pushed my way through the crowd. I made it to the rear door in time to witness two men and a woman being hustled out, sacks over their heads and hands tied behind their backs. Realizing too late I was in over my head and I had already seen too much, I tried to back away, but I was exposed in the small hall and not hidden by the crowds.

Emrick was coming up the rear of the group, hoodie pulled over his head and hands shoved in his pockets. He stopped before leaving, his hand holding the heavy metal door, and turned slowly to see me standing there, hands clasped over my mouth.

I was such a fool.

His face was hidden in shadow, and at this moment, he was a dark, faceless entity which couldn't be reasoned with. When I heard his demand, I tried to run, but I was too slow.

"Take her."

Shrieking as a sack was pulled over my head, I was bundled up, my kicking and screaming doing nothing to stop them as I was thrown into the back of a van, landing on top of a stranger's body.

Muttering to myself, I managed to roll over until I hit the cold metal side of the van with a thud. At least I was no longer lying on top of other people. Tearing the sack from my head, I tried to stand but was immediately thrown into the side of the van again as it took off and rounded the first corner out of the back alleyway. The three people on the van's floor had their wrists tied and were lying uncomfortably on top of each other, sacks still in place on their heads and groaning with every turn.

Crawling, I managed to pull myself to the front of the van despite the violent steering. Emrick was driving like a madman—it was a wonder he could see at this time of night with those dark sunglasses on. He didn't look at me as I clambered into the passenger seat and pulled the seat belt on with a click, and he shifted gears as the van screeched in protest to his rough treatment.

"Where are you taking me?"

His head swiveled toward me, his expression blank, still half hidden in shadows under his hood. He said nothing, looked back at the road, and continued to drive.

"Where are you *taking* me?" I asked, raising my voice over the van's rumbling and trying to get a rise out of Emrick, anything from him besides a cold stare.

"Shut up."

When I moved to lean across him and grab the wheel, his hand shot out and grabbed my throat. He wasn't looking at me and kept his gaze firmly ahead as he guided me back into my seat, using his grip to maneuver me.

"Who are they?"

He didn't answer.

"Why am I here?"

Nothing.

"Emrick!"

Slamming on the brakes, he pulled to the side of the road, ignoring the car horns as they screamed past and the insults of the people on the sidewalk he had almost hit with his bumper. I bet they wouldn't talk like that if they knew who was behind the tinted windows. With a flick, Emrick undid his seat belt, leaning over me until my back was pressed against the van door, my own seat belt twisted out of shape. He gripped where it met the clasp, covering it with his large hand, and any thoughts I had of undoing it and running were tossed away.

He took his sunglasses off and threw them to the floor. "What do you see?"

"I—"

"Tell me what you *see!*"

Staring at his eyes, his pupils were dilated as they jumped between mine. This close, I could only barely see the difference in color between the black of his pupils and the darkness of his irises.

"I... I don't know."

And it was the truth. I didn't know anymore. I was a fool to think there was anything to him beyond the tales of what he was capable of. He had proven himself to be dangerous, volatile, and violent with a temper which could snap at any second. He shifted wildly between a man who threw someone out of the club to protect me to a man who would drag me down a hall and choke me. Every second in his company was either pleasure or pain, or both.

I coughed as he grabbed my throat, his weight resting awkwardly on me as I pressed against the van's door. He asked again, quieter, "What do you see? *Look. At. Me.*"

The growl when he forced the words out was more animal than human, but I looked at him. I studied his eyes and took a moment to look beyond them. I saw the same things I always did—anger, pain, and a streak of reckless abandon that put everyone around him in danger.

But really, all I could see was his black eyes.

"Nothing," I whispered.

His hand retracted from my neck, and Emrick stared at me for a beat longer before returning to his seat. "That's right," he muttered, pulling the van back into the traffic. "Nothing."

We drove for hours, and I littered him with questions about the people in the back, who had gone silent since our heated exchange, all of which Emrick ignored. This wasn't a surprise to me, but I needed to keep talking. Obviously, it was overstepping a major boundary by going out back when he was dealing with business, a call I wondered if I was going to pay for with my life.

Yet, for some reason I couldn't explain, I didn't feel fear. Anxious, yes. But not fear for my life. Was there still hope in me there was good in Emrick and he wouldn't kill me? Or had I simply resigned myself and accepted my fate?

We left the city boundaries, and I sighed, leaning my head against the cool window and staring outside as my breath fogged up the glass. I did say I wanted to leave this city one way or another.

I'd prefer it not to be this way, though.

Twisting my lips, I sighed again. Well, I had wanted to see what Emrick was capable of with my own eyes, and I guess now I was going to see it up close and personal. I should be more concerned, panicking and yanking at the door handle. My eyes flickered to the door, and I almost laughed out loud when I saw both the handle and the winder for the window had been removed from the old van.

To prevent escape. *Clever.*

Maybe if I offered to help him kill these people, he'd let me live.

While it wasn't ideal, I could stomach it. It wouldn't be the first time.

When Emrick finally slowed down, I couldn't have even told you which way I'd need to start walking to get back to the city. Everything beyond the scope of the headlights was black, and he pulled off the road, the van bumping uncomfortably over the uneven terrain before he came to a stop.

Leaving the headlights on, he stepped out, slamming the door behind him. Scrambling to undo my seat belt, I awkwardly shifted over his seat and out the driver's side door, racing around the van as he dragged out the people from the back. Tugging them by their clothes, he dropped them into the dirt. First, the two men, then the woman. They had already begun begging for their lives as they were moved from the van, and one by one, Emrick roughly lifted them to their feet, shouting at them when they took a moment to find their footing on the uneven ground before yanking the sacks from their heads.

When he slid a gun out of his back pocket, on instinct, I cried out, "Wait!"

He didn't stop, checking the bullets and sliding the cartridge back in with a click.

But his hands were shaking.

Surely, he'd done this countless times before, so why was killing an issue now?

Aww, hell, I had to try again. The pull to this man was too strong, and no matter what he did to me, all his back-and-forth bullshit, I had to try. There wasn't *nothing* in his eyes, there was fear and pain, and if I were here to save him from doing something he'd rather not do, then maybe it would start to redeem me for what *I* had done.

Selfish, seeking redemption through saving another, but some childish, perhaps foolish part of me, thought maybe we had been brought together for a reason.

Did I believe in fate? I didn't even know anymore. I had my path laid out before me, a glittery gold road that led out of this city and away from my past. Until him, until I saw in his eyes the same thing I saw reflected in mine when I stared in the mirror. I could go back and forth all day with myself, trying to convince myself to give up and move on. But it was too late, he was intertwined with me now, in my mind. Giving up on Emrick would feel like giving up on myself.

Whatever these people had done, there were other ways he could deal with them.

"Emrick..." I cautiously approached him, placing a hand on top of his when he kept the gun down and his face tilted toward the ground. "You don't have to do this."

He moved so fast.

Flinching as the cold metal of the barrel was pushed against my forehead, I held his eye contact. "What do you know of what I have to do?" he growled out.

"Is that why I'm here, Emrick? You're going to kill me?" Somehow, I was able to keep my voice steady. Did I hold that much faith in the man in front of me? My heart rate increased as I followed his arm with my gaze until his hand was too close to focus on, and the gun was nothing but a black blur between my eyes. With only the moonlight and the glow of the headlights around the front of the van, I could barely see Emrick's face, impossible to tell what he was thinking.

He pushed on the gun, and it dug into my skin. "Did you know what he was when you fucked him?"

His question took me completely off guard, and I fumbled for a moment to find the words. In my head, I had played out a number of things to say and ways he could respond. Yet what he had asked me wasn't even close to anything I had considered him asking. "W-What?"

"Did you know he was a demon? Did the danger excite you?"

There was so much rage in his expression, rage which seemed to flower from nowhere, and within seconds, it was consuming his entire being. From the moment he looked at me, it bubbled to the surface and took over. He *hated* me, he loathed the very ground I walked on, and yet, I had no idea why. "I... I don't know what you're talking about," I stuttered, "Demon? What—"

"Shut *up*." He enunciated the word with another push on the gun. "Shut the fuck up."

His expression was flickering between conflicting emotions, and I knew that look. I knew it because that used to be me, and maybe still was— perhaps I simply denied it. Maybe my imagined connection to Emrick was my internal monologue telling me it was sick of hiding, and I needed to be who I really was. Civil society wasn't for me. I was all shades of messed up. Emrick watched me with haunted eyes, eyes of someone who simply wanted the world to burn and go down screaming with it, taking pleasure in knowing he was part of the downfall. What exactly he was struggling with, I couldn't be sure, but his face read of a man who was falling apart inside.

He was me. I'd been there. I was there. Maybe I never quite escaped from that dark place.

These people may have been the final straw, or whatever they had been involved in, but they were far from the cause of his anger. He was holding so many things inside. I'd like to say I knew what it was like because I had done it and come through the other side, but the truth was I was still stuck there too. Hell, I had thrown myself into the middle of a situation which could have, and still might, kill me, all because I saw pain in the eyes of someone and hoped their darkness matched mine. I was begging for a connection with someone like me, so I knew I wasn't alone in this world.

"Emrick..." I tried not to sigh too loudly when the gun was removed from my head, and he pointed it toward the three he had dragged from the van. They immediately started pleading and begging for their lives.

"What did they do?" I whispered, finding my voice. "Why do they deserve this?"

"They are just pawns." He was staring past me as though I was no longer there but simply a voice in his head. "But they destroyed what was mine."

"Will they do it again?"

The woman moved to step forward, halting when the gun shifted to her. "Please..." She looked at me. "We were paid to do a job. We won't do it again… we needed the money. Please, you have to believe us."

Pressing my lips into a thin line, I watched her face. She wasn't crying, but she looked close to snapping the thread of control she had left. I still didn't know why I was here, perhaps Emrick *wanted* to be talked out of it.

Or maybe he wanted a witness.

He didn't have to grab me at the club, what I had seen had hardly been incriminating, but why that should bother him, I don't know. They could have knocked me out, fired me, or simply shoved me back into the crowd and told me to get back to work. But he didn't, he brought me with him.

What do you see?

What had he been hoping I would see?

Maybe there was a flicker of light left in him yet. Lord knows I was hardly the person to bring someone back onto the right path, but right here and now, he needed help. Maybe I could offer that help.

"Emrick…" I whispered. "Let them go." He said nothing and didn't move. I wished I could tell what was going on in his head. "You don't have to do this, you're better than this."

Finally, his eyes shifted to mine, and the gun lowered, only slightly. His would-be victims were still wary of the weapon as they should be. We weren't out of this yet.

"I'm not better than this."

"You are." Moving in front of him, I placed a hand on his and pushed until the gun was pointing at the ground. "You're the sort of man who kicks someone out of a club for hitting a woman." I kept my voice quiet, so only he could hear me. I knew the importance of his reputation, and despite how he had been treating me, he obviously needed help. All I could do was hope him bringing me along was his way of asking for it and pray I wasn't reading the situation wrong and would pay for my error in judgment with my life.

Assuming it wasn't already his plan to kill me tonight, maybe he wanted to fuck again first.

A shudder moved down my spine, excited when I shouldn't be.

"They can't get away with what they've done," he growled out.

He was protecting his own in the most messed-up way possible. He was protecting what was important to him—his business and his empire—the only things he had in this world. He's putting everything on the line to protect it as I had done with my family.

Where I failed, maybe I can help him succeed.

I know why he needed to kill these people, but perhaps there's another way, a way where he can protect his and keep what was left of his soul.

All I kept thinking was I was doing a terrible job

of abiding by the city's rules—*keep to yourself, keep your head down, and trust no one.*

I had thrown myself into the firing line with him. Maybe *for* him.

"I know they can't..." I said. "But maybe a warning instead of death." Turning, I looked at them. They were all watching me intently, trying to figure out how I fit into this equation. "They are pawns as you said. They're not the ones who need punishment."

The corner of his lip twitched, and I thought he was going to smile. "You could get a job doing this."

"No, I'm not cut out for this industry."

He stared at me with those eyes so dark, reflecting the moon. "I wouldn't be so sure of that."

Could he see the darkness inside me?

Like recognizing like.

A flicker of something sparked inside me, the smallest part that made me feel like I had found a *place* in this city, something I had never had before. A place with him.

What would it feel like to run an empire like that?

Touching my fingers gently to the gun's cold metal, I shuddered again. There was so much power in that weapon, so much power in Emrick. Did I trust myself to hold that power again? Emrick was staring at the three people in front of him, and when I managed to slide the gun from his grip, their stance relaxed.

Until I pointed the weapon at them again.

"There's another way, Emrick," I muttered, my hands steady and arms outstretched in front of me. "You don't need to kill."

The confusion was evident in the strangers' faces until a shot rang out into the silent night, the sound disappearing quickly over the flat plane with nothing to create reverberations. One of the men fell, clutching his knee and screaming. I knew what I was doing—the part of me I didn't want to acknowledge knew at least. Sometimes it was as though there were two people inside me, but since meeting Emrick, those two people were starting to merge.

The shot was directly to his knee.

He'd be able to walk again, one day.

Maybe.

Unlikely.

But that wasn't my problem.

The woman dropped to her knees beside the man, throwing a terrified glance at me, as though she had been expecting me to protect her.

She had no idea that I did.

I just saved their lives.

"Go," Emrick said.

The woman's lip trembled. "Where?"

"I don't care. Away from my city, away from me. You stay the fuck out of *my* city because I swear, if you're ever seen there again, you won't get another chance." Emrick glanced at me, and I lifted the gun again in warning before Emrick approached them. The man on the ground cowered, and when Emrick dug his thumb into the bullet wound, he screamed anew. Emrick continued talking as if nothing had happened, blood spurting out of the wound onto his hand and the man's jeans. "Don't ever speak of me, or *her*, to anyone. Now *go.*"

The two of them helped their injured friend, supporting him between them and together they hobbled away and disappeared into the darkness.

Snatching the gun from me without looking at my face, he flicked the safety on before stashing the gun back in his pants, and I released a pent-up sigh.

Emrick started pacing as the silence grew around us, running his fingers through his hair and muttering to himself, "That was a mistake."

"No, it wasn't."

"It was a mistake to bring you."

"Why *did* you bring me?"

He didn't answer and continued his pacing. Then repeated, "It was a mistake to let them go."

"No, it wasn't."

He was on me, gripping my face and smearing his victim's blood on my cheek and neck. It was still warm, but I didn't flinch. "What would you know of this life?"

"More than you think!" I spat. "I *know* what it's like to crave violence, to feel that power of a gun, death at my fingertips. Don't assume you're the only one here who knows that feeling." When he said nothing and continued to stare into my eyes, I dropped my voice. "It wasn't a mistake. Killing for killing's sake isn't good for the soul. They were just pawns, as you said. Besides, it's not like they got away without warning."

He laughed then, a dark laugh without humor, and I flinched under his touch. He paused, and his grip turned into a caress as he ran his thumb along my cheek. I must look a mess with a stranger's blood smeared on my face, and I felt I should care more. But Emrick's eyes were on mine, blazing bright in the night with an intensity I hadn't seen before.

"What's in your past? What did you do?" he asked quietly.

"Nothing."

He chuckled then. "Liar."

I trembled under his touch, his warmth had the memories flaring in me. Those memories of long ago—of violence and sex—blended with those thoughts of the other night with Emrick as he penetrated me, and I felt myself getting wet.

What was he doing to me? What was I doing to *myself?*

Emrick's face was lit with a sinister grin, knowing the effect he was having on me. "Maybe you're just as dark as me."

"I'm trying not to be."

"But you can't help it, can you? It's in you, and it's always there, eating away at your insides, filling your head with thoughts you don't want to have. But now you're so conditioned to think there's something wrong with you, you can't help but fight it. I think that's why you fought being with me, not because you didn't want to but because you were afraid I'd bring it out of you."

How did he know?

"Emrick—"

His mouth met mine in an explosion of sensation. His lips were so soft in contrast to his rough touch, and he eased me into the kiss, sliding his tongue into my mouth only when I parted my lips and welcomed the intrusion. I moaned against his mouth. He was so hot, his body pressed against mine as his other hand snaked up my back and tangled in my hair. Using his weight, he pushed against me until I was forced to kneel and then lie in the dirt as he lay on top of me, fucking my mouth with his tongue. Wet, hot, and dirty, he took control as he did in the bedroom, and his lips worked expertly against mine.

I gasped when he pulled away, and he maintained his grip on my hair, his lips a whisper from mine. "Tell me..." he murmured. "What do you see?"

Studying his eyes, darker than the night as he

stared hard at me, my lips were swollen from his assault, and I ached for more. I didn't know what he wanted me to say, he was, as always, almost impossible to read. So, all I could do was tell him the truth of what I saw in those eyes beyond the darkness that emulates mine, beyond the anger, and beyond the front that he puts on. I saw in the way his hand shook when he held the gun, even though I'm certain he'd held it still countless times before and followed through. I saw it flash deeper and darker when he yelled, and at its strongest when he was kicking me out of his bedroom for reasons I still don't understand.

"Pain," I whispered.

His lips met mine again, and for the briefest of moments before his touch became rough, there was a gentle caress, where his tongue played with mine rather than dominating me, he kissed me in a way a lover would. But the moment was shattered when he hungrily devoured my mouth again, nipping and biting at my lips, and I thought he was going to take me right here in the dirt in the middle of nowhere.

I knew then, he wanted me to make him do the right thing. He *wants* me in a way he doesn't want to admit to himself, in the same way I'm struggling to admit how badly I want him. Because when I think of him while I'm haunted by thoughts of him on top of me like this—but naked with his cock driving into me over and over again—I also think of standing beside him on that balcony, looking out over our empire.

The rush of power was insatiable. I'd felt it before, having someone kneel at your feet and beg for their life, and I wanted *more*.

The rush of violence and sex, it shouldn't work for me, but it just *did*.

Because I was just as messed up as him, but he simply owned it.

Emrick brought out the worst in me, and maybe I salvaged a small, good part of him.

What did that make us together? One messed-up unit.

When he broke away from me, his expression was unreadable again. He glanced between his hand and my cheek before running his hand down my face from my forehead to chin, smearing my skin with blood, then taking my top in both hands and using the fabric to finish wiping the blood and dirt from his fingers.

My lip curled in disgust, and there was a slight smirk when he looked down at me as he stood. "I'll tell the boys I taught you a lesson so you know not to step out of line again."

I didn't know what to say, so I simply whispered, "Okay." I brushed myself off before following him back to the van.

CHAPTER
14

EMRICK

What does she see?

Pain.

Obviously, she sees something I can't. It's been far too long living in the darkness. I've made the dark my entire life. Sleeping through the day when I need to and being active at night. Embracing the darkness inside me and molding my world outside to suit it.

Everything was taken from me, and instead of understanding my revenge, they took my wings too. There's nothing left of the old Emrick, not a shred of who I used to be. All that remains is the darkness inside, the selfish need to protect my own as long as that included me, for I'd throw any of these men under a train if it meant sparing my own life.

Somehow, Cara knew I didn't want to kill those

people. I reached out and dragged her down the rabbit hole with me, and she came through. Killing is not something I take lightly, no matter what everyone thinks of me. If I can avoid it, I will, and in the instances where it is absolutely necessary, often I'll be a coward and leave it to someone else.

Not those first men, though, the ones I killed which led to my wings being taken. I took great pleasure in that act. When the street was stained with splatters of their blood, and it was washing away in the rain and down the gutter, I had no regrets.

No regrets, except that I couldn't go back to save Emily. No amount of celestial magic could turn back time or bring back the dead.

Was Cara my second chance? My redemption? A rare diamond who not only saw past my darkness but felt it within her too. I'd be bad for her if she already struggled with internal conflict, being around me would only make it worse. I didn't even know what it was she was hiding. Would she tell me if I pushed her? Did she trust me enough to?

She had no reason to, and I don't blame her. Trusting me would be poor judgment.

And as petty as it seemed, I could not get past the fact she was tainted—touched by a demon, *fucked* by a demon. I simply couldn't forgive her for that.

Standing abruptly, Tate glanced up at me, shifting his eyes away from the activity on the dance floor and in the bar. He was watching Cara, and I had been trying to avoid doing exactly that all night. When we returned early this morning and I shoved her through the back doorway, Tate was waiting. She had stumbled and fallen near his feet, looking up at him, her eyes wide, and her face and clothes smeared in blood and dirt.

Tate simply raised an eyebrow at me as she scrambled to her feet and ran away, and I lifted a shoulder. He asked no questions.

But tonight he was watching her closely, and she had not cast a single glance up to the balcony. Whether from respect or fear, I wasn't sure.

It hardly mattered. I needed to get my head back in the game. Someone inside this building was trying to bring me down, had even gone as far as hiring people to destroy my properties. I'd spent the day going over potentials, looking into the files I kept on everyone, trying to find a weak spot someone could use to exploit them. Or perhaps something that would lead them to try to take what's mine. I was no closer to figuring out who it was, and as much as I'd throw them all under the bus, they would do the same to me. Loyalty only stretched so far, and as long as they were paid and kept in a lifestyle they enjoyed while being able to play out their violent desires, they had no need to overthrow me.

No, something deeper was going on here.

Targeting Spicy had been a mistake because that only *confirmed* it was an inside job, as no one else could have known it was one of my venues.

So now, everyone was on my shit list.

I had work to do to uncover the traitor, but before that, I needed to get Cara's demon-fuck betrayal out of my head, and that meant calling in a long overdue favor.

When she opened the door this time, she was more cautious. Given the last time I was here, I had grabbed her the second I could fit my arm through the door, her caution wasn't only understandable but smart.

"Emrick," she said, her tone deadpan.

"Ray."

Ray was leaning against the door, keeping it open only a crack so I could see her face. She knew what I was and could feel the flicker of celestial power that lived within me and hadn't died just yet. I hoped the fact I wasn't breaking the door down, prying it from her grip and slamming the wood panel into her face was an olive branch.

Because she knew I could do it.

Fallen angel.
Dangerous.
Can't be trusted.
Murderer.
"Can I come in?"

She frowned at me as if unsure why I was asking. It felt strange, and I hadn't realized I was asking until the words had already escaped. I don't *ask* for permission, I *take.*

How long had it been since I asked like that?

"I'd rather you didn't," she said.

Sliding my sunglasses off, I stared into her eyes, leaning one hand on the doorframe and the other on the door. "Let me in, or I'll break this door off its hinges." So much for the olive branch.

She stood back. "All right, all right, you're all about the drama, aren't you?"

Ilsa was sitting on the couch, reading, but she tossed her book to the side and scrambled to her feet when I came in.

I held up a hand. "I'm not here to fight."

"Why *are* you here?"

"Aren't you going to offer me a drink?"

Ray pulled a face. "Sure. Emrick, would you like a nice tall glass of tell-me-why-the-fuck-you're-here?"

I wasn't in the mood for her shit. "It's time to pay back the favor you owe me."

"I don't owe you shit." Ray kept her voice level

and calm while Ilsa shouted, *"Fuck you,"* from behind me. Bonding with a demon had made her into a loose cannon. From the way I remember it, Ilsa used to be the level-headed one.

"I need you to track someone for me..." I kept talking as though she hadn't responded, "... a demon."

"So find yourself a bounty hunter."

Stepping closer to Ray, she stood her ground, but her eyes flashed yellow in irritation as I invaded her space. "I'm asking *you*."

My anger was bubbling beneath the surface. I had something that needed doing so I could stop thinking about it. There was too much going on with the business and within me to deal with right now. I'd spend the best part of the decade in a state of perpetual numbness, allowing only the strength of my anger at the injustice of my falling to carry me through.

Then all this shit with a traitor, and on top of that, *she* had come along and insisted there was more within me.

Had Cara seen something there, or was she only hoping? Another pathetic human trying to see the best in everyone. She had the darkness within her, something in her past I had yet to unravel. Maybe she was hoping if someone like me could be saved, then she could be too.

Maybe she was trying to redeem her own shit by

saving me.

"Who are they?" Ray asked, crossing her arms over her ample chest.

"How the fuck am I supposed to know?" The words exploded from me as I threw my arms up in the air. "I just need to know who tainted her, so I can kill them," I growled out, pushing the words through clenched teeth.

Ilsa had gone silent, and Ray's eyebrows were raised.

"Wha—"

"You fucking demons..." When I got into Ray's space again, Ilsa growled but kept her distance for now. Ray hissed at me as I jammed a finger against her chest. "You think you can do whatever the fuck you like, don't you? You fuck, fight, kill, and party without *any* consequence. You think you can take just *anybody* you want! Demons took everything from me, and you can't have *her!*"

She simply watched me as I heaved through the breaths, each one that filled my lungs was painful. Ray's expression had softened, and she had dropped her arms to her sides, not even looking at where I was touching her, still pointing my finger against her chest in accusation, trembling slightly with the rage that threatened to consume me whole. I was barely holding on as it was.

"All right," she said. "You're going to have to explain that little outburst."

Ilsa side-stepped me as if I were poisonous when I stormed past and dropped myself onto the couch.

Perhaps I was.

Ray sat next to me in what I thought was a bold move. If she weren't afraid of me anymore, I'd need to do something to change that. I couldn't lose grip on the world I had built because one woman had gotten into my head.

"She fucked a demon, I can taste it on her. Your *stink* fucking lingers." I glanced at her out of the corner of my eye, and she seemed unaffected by my insult.

"What does he mean?" Ilsa asked.

"Demons' leave a mark, like a scent, because of our pheromones. It's pretty potent. Humans won't notice it but other demons..." she glanced at me, "... or angels will."

"Do I have it?"

Ray stared at her partner, lust flashing in her eyes. "Oh yeah, my scent is all over you. A demon or angel would smell you a mile away." She turned back to me. "But you said she fucked him... how long ago? Could've been years, right?"

I lifted a shoulder, not willing to commit to an answer. She was right. The scent was so faint, it was barely there. But it *was* there.

Fucking demons.

Every time I thought of them, the hate pulsed through my veins thick and strong. The hatred is what kept me going for years. Hatred and anger covered the pain, and it was a perfect covering. But when someone starts to peel back those layers, the pain pushes its way through, reminding me I'm not as immune to it as I thought I was.

And reminding me if I were privy to the same rules as demons, I'd still be an angel.

Then the one person who sees something in my eyes past the black, who sees the pain, is just one more thing demons tainted and took from me. Ray flinched when my anger peaked. She could see it on my face with the way my jaw clenched and feel it in the air between us.

Good, I wanted her to be afraid of me. Fear was all I had now.

"So, let's see if I have this straight," Ray said, slapping her hands on her knees. "You want me to sniff your girlfriend's pussy for traces of a demon she fucked years ago and then find and kill him, yes?"

When my hand found her throat, she flinched again but made no attempt to stop me. Her eyes flared yellow as I growled, "Do not talk about her like that." I had barely finished my sentence before I felt the silver against my neck, turning slightly to see Ilsa holding a blade to my skin.

"I know this won't kill you..." she said, her voice the even-controlled tone I remembered from when we first met, "... but it'll still hurt like a bitch if I drive it through your neck. *Let her go.*"

Ray and I held each other's gaze, she knew as well as I a blade through the neck—silver or not—would almost definitely kill me, but apparently Ilsa didn't understand how being fallen changed me. Dropping my hand from Ray's neck, Ilsa moved the blade from mine and took a step back.

"I can't help you, Emrick." Ray watched me. "But I think you knew that already." After a pause, she asked, "Why do you hate demons so much?"

I threw a look at her with all the hate I could muster and stood, straightening my outer jacket before throwing the hood over my head and turning to leave. With my hand on the doorknob, I turned back. Ray was still sitting, staring at me, and waiting for an answer to her question.

"I know of demons who've killed humans and still live on Earth," I muttered, letting my dark eyes fixate on Ray. She was one of *them*, and while she may not have killed, she was no better than the rest. I once thought I saw myself in her, watching her compassion and affection for this human, but a demon was a demon. "When I killed the men who killed the woman I loved, I lost my wings." Ray's face changed when she saw the tear that escaped before I could swipe it away. "You tell me how that's justice."

I left, slamming the door behind me.

When there was a knock on the door, and Sven pulled it open, Tate's eyes shot to me immediately after taking in Cara standing in the doorway. She was carrying a tray with vodka and glasses, and I felt the frown deepen on my forehead. I hadn't ordered anything. Steadfastly ignoring Tate's gaze on me, I waved my hand at him, and after a beat, he and Sven stalked out the door, pulling it closed behind them.

"Cara."

Her brows creased together. "Emrick," she said, mimicking my deadpan tone. "Thought you might like a drink."

"I didn't order anything."

"I know." She poured a generous glass and handed it to me, her hand hovering between us as we both stared at the glass. Cara pouted, placing the glass I had refused to accept on the table before standing, awkwardness taking over her at my stare.

"Why are you here, Cara?"

Her frown deepened. "You know what? I don't even know. Whatever I was thinking, I guess I was wrong."

I was on my feet, grabbed her arm, and spun her

to face me. Her hands came up between us, pressing against my chest. "Why are you here?" I growled.

"Nothing, never mind."

"You have to stay away from me."

"You *kissed* me."

Dropping my chin to my chest, I increased my grip on her arm when she went to pull away, wrapping my other arm around her and pulling her against me, loving the way her fingers gripped against my clothes. Her nails were digging into me, bringing me the sweet pain I craved. I could make her hurt, and I wanted the same from her.

But she had already seen too much of me.

"I'm bad for you... you need to stay away from me."

"This is ridiculous, *you* came on to *me.*"

"We fucked. That's all there is to it."

She looked as though I had slapped her, and she knew I was lying. There was more to this, but I couldn't admit it to her, not now.

Not ever.

Snatching her hand out of the air as she moved to touch my face, I stared her down over my glasses. She glared at me, and I could feel the anger pulsing within her. "What do you *see?*" She pushed the words through clenched teeth.

"Anger," I said.

Yanking herself out of my grip, she stepped away from me. "That's right."

She stomped out of the door like a teenager throwing a tantrum, and despite the conflicting emotions shifting through me, I couldn't help but smirk. The image of her lying across my lap while I spanked the disobedience out of her made my cock swell.

I needed to throw myself back into my business.

Turning on my heel, I stormed through the back door into the office and locked it behind me. The entire club was rigged with cameras. Of course, everyone knew that, but I didn't trust any of the people in this building, not fully. Not the men who worked for me, not the staff downstairs, none of the humans on the dance floor. Not a single one of them.

So, in addition to the system you could see was one you could not.

Flicking open my laptop, I logged into the secure system. The people who had set it up were no longer in the city—I paid them a handsome sum, and them disappearing was part of the deal. No leaks.

Scanning through the security footage, I sat for hours waiting for something that would prove who was betraying me. The bottle of vodka I had opened was half empty when I found it.

I don't know how they got into the office and how they knew where to look for the information on my businesses.

But they would answer my questions themselves.

Got you.

CHAPTER
15

CARA

"You know what? This isn't going to fly."

These were the words I muttered to no one in particular, and I guess I was trying to convince myself more than I realized. It sounded more convincing in my head, and as soon as I spoke the words out loud—even if I was only mumbling them to myself as I served—it became apparent I was well out of my depth.

But here's the thing—I no longer cared.

Because I came to Urban to make some cash and start a new life, the details of which I was still figuring out, but I knew it was away from *here*. Then I saw Emrick, and I mean, I really *saw* him, and saw the pain in his eyes and knew it reflected my own. Except where I covered up mine with denial, he covered his with rage, taking it out on a world he felt had wronged him. Not to mention the anger he released on anyone who ended up underneath him in his bedroom.

My clit throbbed at the memory, and I chastised myself. That's not what this was about.

This was about a man who had reached out to me to stop him from doing something he'd regret, something maybe he didn't have it in him to do, and then pushed me away harder than he had the night we were together. I still hadn't figured out what his problem was that night, which was something else I needed to take up with him.

So, enough of this second-guessing.

Because whatever it was that sparked between us, the electricity that shocked us both when we got too close was worth investigating. Then he *kissed* me like *that.*

Maddie wasn't here tonight to talk me out of it, not that she had successfully managed to talk me out of this any step along the way, but I was too agitated to deal with her tonight. She kept telling me the same things over and over again, things I already knew about how dangerous Emrick was, things I no longer cared about because even Maddie didn't know what *I* was capable of.

Grabbing a tray, I loaded it up and stomped up the stairs. Reaching the top, I was hindered access by one of Emrick's men. I didn't know his name, but he looked as though he was a rat turned into human form with his long thin face and eyes that darted around the narrow staircase as though enemies were going to creep through the cracks in the walls.

"Drinks for Emrick," I stated.

He eyed me, then raised a brow. "I see glasses, but I see no drinks."

Somehow I managed to keep myself from cringing. "Look, he asked to see me, the drinks are a cover, and I fucked up, okay?" The curse sounded odd in my mouth, but if I wanted to act the part, I needed to pull it off. It may be strange, but swearing beyond *hell* was something I rarely did, if ever, and I'm not even sure why.

Scratch that, I know *exactly* why I didn't like to swear.

Keep those dirty words out of your mouth, or I'll show you what that mouth can do.

Shuddering, I pushed the memory of the sick voice from my mind. The guard must have seen my expression harden, and his other brow arched to match the first. All I could do was hope he had seen Emrick and me together or was one of the men in the room the night I slinked out.

Or maybe he was new and stupid.

Or both.

"Whatever," he said, rolling his eyes. I frowned as he let me through into the empty balcony. Despite my being pleased at being able to get through, I'd have to tell Emrick how easy it was to talk my way past. That guy had no business working for a man like Emrick if he wasn't going to ask more questions than that.

Placing the tray quietly on the glass coffee table, I approached the door to the office. Turning the knob, I wasn't surprised to find it locked. Steeling myself, I knocked and waited. The door swung open, Emrick's eyes darkened when he saw me, and I took a step back from him, my gaze immediately shot over his shoulder. Choking back a cough, I locked eyes with her as she screamed at me past the gag.

"Maddie?" I cried, raising a hand to my mouth.

Emrick's grip on my upper arm was painful as he yanked me forward into the office and slammed the door behind us, spinning me into the room before I took a few steps to correct myself. His chest was heaving with strained breaths as he watched me, and I backed up a few steps before turning and racing to Maddie, pulling the gag from her mouth.

"Maddie, what's going on?"

"Help me, Cara. This isn't some fucked-up sex game, he's going to kill me!"

She was strapped spread-eagle to some sort of X-shaped rack. I'd never seen anything like it before, and while it looked crude and homemade, I imagined it was part of the effect. Thick bronze brackets were screwed crudely into the dark wood, and the leather straps which held her wrists and ankles cut painfully into her skin.

"You gotta get me out of here." She was yanking forward against the restraints, her dress only partially intact and bra visible. There were angry red marks across her arms and legs, and I wondered what Emrick had done to her.

Or what she had done to deserve it.

It pained me that one of my first thoughts was wondering what she had done, but it was true. He wouldn't have brought her here for no reason, and by her own admission, it wasn't some *sex game,* the idea of which flared something dark and ugly inside me, something that very closely resembled jealousy.

But I couldn't allow myself to feel that, not over Emrick.

"What did you do?" I whispered.

"What did *I* do?" Her voice was hysterical, rising with every syllable. "Why do you assume it's something I've *done?* He's out of his *fucking mind!*"

Emrick came up behind me, sliding an arm around my waist and whispering in my ear, "She's a traitor. Want to shoot her in the kneecap?"

Purposefully, I moved out of his grasp. I didn't need him influencing me. He brought out something in me I was fighting a losing battle to keep hidden. As I kept my eyes on Maddie, he let his arms fall heavily to his sides, and the telltale snarl that escaped his lips was due to my defiance. I had a bone to pick with him, but apparently, that would have to wait. He wasn't to touch me until I had my say.

Because I knew I was going to let him touch me.

Did that make me a sick person? He had my friend tied up and screaming for freedom, apparently beaten, and all I could think of was sex. But his scent was intoxicating me, and while my anger was dissipating and being replaced with confusion and a snippet of fear, it was hard not to get swept up in the feel of him when he was this close. His hard chest, those sculpted arms, the thought of his hands on my body and spanking me into submission, the way he fucked my mouth until I couldn't breathe...

Sex and violence.

"Are you two together or something?" Maddie spat.

"No," we cried in unison, my voice rising an octave in the denial of my interest in him and his a low growl while he eyed me, having lost interest in Maddie when I'd entered the office.

I rubbed my upper arm. "It's complicated."

Maddie laughed, a single sound without humor. "He's a fucking psychopath, Cara! He literally has me *tied up.* What's *wrong with you?* You fucking bitch!" she cried out after Emrick crossed the space between them in a few steps and laid into her with his belt, adding to the angry red marks already crisscrossing her arms and legs.

Approaching Emrick, I placed a hand on his shoulder. He turned on me, raising the belt above his head. I managed to fight back the urge to flinch and waited until he lowered his arm. Moving to the giant X keeping Maddie imprisoned, I laid a hand on her arm, and she hissed where I touched one of the fresh red marks, blood spotting on her skin. "Maddie..." I said, keeping my voice as even as possible. "What did you do?"

"I did it for the money, *all right?* Just tell him to let me go. You obviously have some sort of bond with the dog."

This time Emrick didn't stop when I touched his arm, and swung the belt back and forth, ignoring Maddie's cries as he planted blow after blow across the exposed skin of her arms and legs, ending with a final few on her chest.

Curling my fingers into my hair, I cried at him to stop, and when he finally did, I could practically see the muscles rippling under his clothes as he struggled to keep himself in control. Part of me wondered what he'd be doing if I hadn't come in.

Hopefully, not touching her the way he touched me.

No, he wouldn't. Not with the rage that was so clearly plastered across his features.

"What did you *do?*" I screamed at Maddie. I didn't understand what I had walked in on, and neither of their attitudes was helping me decipher the situation.

"She stole from me." Emrick pointed an accusing finger at her, his arm shaking. "She stole information on my venues, and they've been taking them down one by one."

"Maddie? Is this true?"

"Why do you care, Cara? How deep are you in with this guy?"

"I'm not—"

"Whatever. Yes, I stole from him. I was offered a *huge* sum of money to get information on all his venues, the security systems, the people who work there, everything. So, I broke into his office and took it. Only a little bit at a time so he wouldn't notice."

"Why not take copies?"

Emrick flashed me a warning glare at the question I asked, and Maddie rolled her eyes.

"God, how can you be so naïve? To plant distrust. If things are not only being destroyed, but *going missing*, then how can his workers trust him?"

"You're trying to tear me down from the inside?" Emrick grunted.

"Not me, I'm only in it for the money."

"Who?" he barked.

Maddie shrugged as much as she could in her restraints. "I don't know. I just get the calls, the money, and do the dirty work."

"Maddie, *why?*" I groaned, running my hands

down my face.

"Why do you think? The *money.* You think you're the only one who wants to get out of this city?"

A loud slam from a drawer closing gained our attention as Emrick came back toward us, his gaze fixed hard on Maddie as her eyes widened in fear, and she began to struggle anew against the leather cuffs. Emrick slid a single bullet into the chamber of the revolver, snapping it shut and spinning it before placing the barrel of the gun against Maddie's head.

"Who do you work for?" he pushed out through gritted teeth.

"I don't know," she whispered.

Click.

Maddie moaned with fear as he spun the chamber again before placing the gun back against her temple. "How long do you think you have until your luck runs out?"

"Emrick, *please*... don't do this." He froze at my plea but didn't remove the gun from Maddie's head. "You don't have to do this. She's not a bad person. She only did it for the money."

The gun fell to the floor with a clatter, and Emrick's head turned to survey me over his shoulder. Moving slowly, like a cat stalking its prey, he approached me, and that was somehow more terrifying than the way he could cross a room in a heartbeat, his stride eating the floor beneath him.

I tilted my chin up as his fingers wrapped around

my throat.

"What do you know of what I have to do?" he pushed out through gritted teeth.

"Do it," I whispered, holding contact with his dark eyes as his grip tightened, his palm pressing painfully against my throat. "Do it. If you can." His lip lifted in a growl, and I reached between us, placing a hand on his cheek, trying not to picture him as a wild animal that might bite me. "I believe there's good in you."

With a roar, he dropped his hands from my throat, scooping up the gun and aiming it at Maddie. With a shot that had me covering my ears with my hands, too late to stop the ringing, I dared not look up after he had fired the gun.

CHAPTER 16

EMRICK

Maddie's head hung over her chest, her hair damp from sweat from my previous ruthless attentions and covering her face.

"Emrick," Cara whispered, the word obscured as her hands covered her mouth.

"Don't say a fucking thing," I hissed at her.

Maddie groaned, lifting her head to reveal the tears streaming down her face as I paused, listening for a break in the music after the gunshot. As expected, there was none. The DJ, like the others who worked here, knew better than to investigate any sounds from this office, even if there was now a hole through the wall over my desk. Cara rushed forward to Maddie, undoing the restraints on her ankles and wrists.

"What the fuck do you think you're doing?"

Cara glared at me as she lifted Maddie down from the cross. "She was obviously manipulated, Emrick. Please."

Maddie dry heaved before dissolving into dramatic sobs, gripping onto Cara in a way that made my blood boil, watching her traitorous hands grab onto Cara's shoulders, snagging on the loose tendrils of her hair that had fallen from her ponytail.

"I won't do it again, I swear," Maddie pleaded before having the nerve to turn to me. She was unable to hold my eye contact for long as I stared her down, the gun still warm in my hand. Cara may believe her bullshit, but I didn't. "Please, Emrick, I don't know who hired me, and I won't do it again... please."

"Leave." I grunted out the word.

"What?" Maddie sobbed.

"Leave. I can't let you stay here, not now." When she went to argue, I growled at her. "You're lucky I'm not fucking killing you, bitch." Crossing the room, I snatched at what was left of her clothes. "I should be torturing the answer out of you. So, you leave, or we'll start playing roulette again."

She heaved through another dry sob, an act I wasn't buying at all, before racing past me. I could hear her fighting with the lock, trying to get out while I stared hard at Cara, who hadn't moved, pinned under my gaze.

When the door closed behind Maddie, Cara opened her mouth to speak. "Shut it." Even though she closed her mouth, her jaw tightened against the urge to argue with me. "Don't you *ever* interfere with my business again."

"She's my friend."

"I don't *care.* She stole from me, and she had information."

"She didn't know anything!"

"You don't know that!" I roared at her.

"I *know* Maddie. I've known her forever, and if she said she didn't know anything, she didn't *know* anything. Please, you did the right thing."

There it was, the tiniest flicker of doubt across her perfect features. Was it doubt in me or doubt in her *friend?*

"You keep saying that. Who are you trying to convince there's something worth saving in me? Because I already know the answer you seem to be in denial about."

"There is good in you."

But her voice was small as though her conviction was fading. She was blinking up at me, so close her breasts brushed against my chest. She was aroused, the fabric of her dress doing nothing to hide her hardening nipples, tight little sensitive buds that would make her scream if I sunk my teeth into them. Those wide, innocent eyes, eyes she claimed hid darkness of their own, but I had yet to see real evidence of that beyond a feeling I had about her. All she had tried to do was change who I was to fit some misguided image she had built up in her head.

Worse, she was interfering with my business now. Twice she had made me act in a way I shouldn't, to give people second chances when they had done nothing to prove they deserved it.

Maybe she needed a reminder of who I really was.

When I swept a hand over the back of her neck, her lips pouted, expecting a kiss that never came. I had made a mistake kissing her, but this wasn't about that anymore. The softness she had brought out inside me needed to be stamped down *hard*.

If I were to bring my business back into line, I needed to get Cara out of my system.

My lips met her neck, licking and biting at her skin as she groaned. Before she could lift her hands to touch me, I stepped away.

"Take your clothes off," I snapped.

"What?" she asked, having the nerve to look incredulous at my demand.

"You heard me, take off your clothes."

"Why?"

Her tone was somewhere between defiance, arousal, and confusion, and her facial features reflected the mixture of conflicting emotions. I had pushed her away, and here I was telling her to strip for me, and I didn't give a damn she was confused. I had tried to do the *right thing* by getting her away from me, and she kept forcing herself back into my life.

If she was so damn sure she understood my darkness and she wanted it, then I'd give it to her.

"Because you need to be taught a lesson for continuing to interfere..." I whispered, grabbing her face and squeezing her cheeks together, forcing her lips to pout, "... and because you seem to want me, darkness and all, so I'll give it to you."

And because I needed to feel power again, the power she had taken from me. I felt weak around her because she got into my head, into my mind and soul. She was in every inch of me, and after everything that happened, I didn't like to feel out of control. I made a *choice* to kill those men to avenge Emily, and I made the choice knowing they would take my wings. But where Cara was involved, it felt like I needed her approval more than I needed the power to make a choice. I *cared* what she thought, and I *hated* caring about things, especially about people.

So, I was taking back my power.

Her thighs pressed together as her hands clenched by her sides, and my snarl turned into a grin. She wanted it so fucking badly, the whore. But something flared inside me, a possessiveness I haven't felt since... since Emily. Because I knew Cara didn't want it from just anyone, she wanted *me.* Only me. She kept coming back to *me.* She had seen something dangerous in me, looked beyond it, and she simply kept. Coming. Back.

So be it.

Shoving her back and waiting for her to find her footing, she rubbed her cheeks where I had gripped her, frowning at me even as her cheeks flushed and breathing became rapid. Finding the top of the zipper on the side of her dress, she pulled it down, the widening V exposing more of her to me before she slipped it off her shoulders and let it fall to the floor. Cara stared at me defiantly for a beat longer before reaching back and undoing the clasp of her bra, letting it fall over the pile of fabric that was her dress. Her panties followed shortly after, and she stepped out of the tangle and kicked it to the side.

Cara was keeping her arms to her sides, neither crossing them over her body to hide herself nor placing them on her hips with the attitude I knew she possessed. Shrugging out of my hoodie, I let my eyes wander up and down her naked body.

"Take off your shoes," I barked at her as I pulled my tank over my head and cast it aside.

She bent at the hip to undo the clasp, and I wished I had a view of the other side to see the curves of her ass tempting and teasing me while she finished taking off her heels. Standing again, she simply watched me, her eyes widening when I retrieved my discarded belt, folding it in two and letting the leather slide across my palm.

"Bend over the desk."

"Emrick—"

She jumped when I slapped the belt against my thigh, the harsh slap ricocheting around the room. "Are you going to argue, or are you going to bend over and accept your punishment?"

Her eyes flashed with lust as she rubbed her thighs together again, desperate for friction against her aching clit. I would provide it soon enough, but only when I said so.

She'd come only when *I* allowed it.

"Don't make me repeat myself, Cara."

She shuddered when I said her name, and my lips curled into a satisfied snarl as she bent over the heavy desk, exposing her bare ass to me. Running my hand up her thigh before grasping the cheek, she hummed and moved against my palm.

Crack.

Cara cried out as I landed a blow over her ass with the belt, her pale skin already turning red where I had struck her. The satisfaction I had gotten from inflicting this punishment on Maddie for her betrayal was nothing to how my senses exploded when I did it to Cara. My cock swelled in my pants, begging to be released and claim her. I struck her again, making her scream as I hit the exact spot I had previously. After three more, I stopped to admire the color her skin was taking on, caressing the sensitive area with my palm.

"Spread your legs."

She did so without further argument, and I growled my approval, unzipping my pants and freeing my aching cock from its confines. Grinding into her, she moaned at the mixture of sensations between my cock pressed between her ass cheeks and the rough scrape of the fabric against her already abused skin.

Reaching across her, I opened a drawer, sliding out a letter opener. It looked foreboding but was almost harmless. Although I supposed if you stabbed hard enough, you could kill someone with it.

I didn't know, I hadn't tried.

Yet.

The wooden handle was thick and long, and still leaning over her, I slipped my fingers into her mouth, groaning with her when she began sucking on them like the good girl she is for me. Maneuvering the letter opener's handle between her teeth, I guided her to bite down on it, loving how she obeyed even as she frowned with confusion. When I bit into her neck, she cried out, biting down on the wood. I hoped she dented it, and I was left with the imprint of her teeth marks to remind me of the sweet pleasure and pain she was about to endure.

"You'll need it," I mumbled against her skin,

kissing away the pain from the bite I had just inflicted. She mouthed something around the wood, it sounded like my name, and I hissed air through my teeth with pleasure, still grinding my cock against her ass. Guiding her hands to grip the desk's edges, I chuckled as she shuddered. "Don't let go," I said against her skin before straightening behind her.

When I fisted my cock, guiding the head against her puckered rear entrance, she whined loudly against the wood between her teeth, looking back at me with those wide eyes.

"Surely, you've done this before," I crooned, rubbing the precum from the head of my cock over the entrance to her delicious ass. She did a small nod and shrug combination and mumbled something around the wood which sounded something like *not in a while*. Fine, at least I wasn't taking her virginity, and she was not innocent, or so she claimed.

Spitting on her hole, I pushed the head of my cock in, watching her knuckles turn white as she gripped the desk, throwing the head back and groaning as her teeth clenched down. Waiting a beat before pushing in a bit further, I used my fingers to rub her pussy. She was dripping wet for me, so I dragged some of those juices up and over her ass, coating my cock before shoving the rest of the way in and pushing past that final resistance until I was fully sheathed within her. Cara's ass tightened and clenched around me, and her whimpers were so sweet, music to my ears. Staying still, I gave her time to get used to the intrusion, and I hoped she was grateful for small mercies.

After a short while, she started shifting her hips, trying to grind against the desk to get friction on her clit.

But not yet.

With a palm on her lower back, I stilled her movement, shushing her gently. When I leaned forward, she cried out at the change of angle, and I whispered against her ear, "Not yet, pussycat, but don't you worry." I shushed her again as she began to whimper and moan when I started slowly thrusting into her ass. "I'll make you come so hard you won't be able to stand."

Latching my teeth into her shoulder, she cried out again. I straightened, grabbed her hips and took a moment to enjoy the view of my cock disappearing into her ass before I began thrusting. Long, deep, slow thrusts had her shuddering every time I bottomed out in her ass. Closing my eyes, I tilted my head toward the ceiling, letting my mouth drop open as she clamped around me with each intrusion, harder than the last. *Fuck,* she was so *fucking tight,* gripping me in all the best ways.

Grunting as I thrust into her ass, I let the animalistic growls escape after they rumbled deep in my chest. Her hips might be bruised with how I was gripping them, but I couldn't stop. Reaching around, I snaked my hand between her legs and pinched her swollen clit between my thumb and finger. The letter opener clattered to the desk as she cried out when I began rubbing her clit in small, tight circles. She clenched around me, but it wasn't enough to make me stop, thrusting through the resistance and making her cry out again.

"Come for me, Cara, come while I fuck your tight little ass."

She groaned, gripped the edges of the desk as I kept working her clit, slick with her arousal. She was fucking *loving* it as I took her, and I forced my cock deeper into her, pushing her limits harder than she thought she could handle, but I knew she could take it.

My own orgasm was building, and I wanted to feel her clench around me as I emptied my load into her ass, claiming it as my own as I had with her pussy and mouth. Her arms began to tremble as she neared her peak, and I whispered dirty things in her ear until she was pushed over the edge. As she came, I pinched hard on her clit again, drawing out the ecstasy of the pain, and when my orgasm hit, I leaned forward, gripping her shoulder with my teeth. She cried out and grabbed the desk, clenching around me as I roared, thrusting my cum deep into her ass.

Collapsing on top of her, she was whimpering softly with her cheek pressed on the desk's hard surface.

"Can you stand?" I whispered.

She chuckled. "I think so."

With a growl, I pulled myself out of her ass, tighter after her orgasm. "Then my work isn't done."

She whined again when I kneeled behind her, slamming a palm into her lower back when she went to stand.

"What are you—"

"Shh, pussycat, I'm claiming you. If you want to be mine, I'm going to *make* you mine."

She moaned as I breathed in the scent of her arousal, my mouth next to her wet cunt. My breath hitched as I paused. Her scent was tainted.

But not with *him,* not with the scent of a demon anymore.

But with me.

She smelled like *me.*

My celestial scent had overridden his. I had claimed her, and she was mine now.

Growling deep in my throat, I thrust my tongue into her dripping pussy, gripping her thighs when she jumped and tried to move away. Lapping at her juices, I flicked my tongue over her clit. It had been a long time since I had done this for someone— since I had *wanted* to do this for someone. She tasted so good, and I couldn't help but dip my tongue into her sweet cunt every now and then before returning my attention to her clit. When her leg began to twitch, I grinned against her, sucking hard on that sweet clit of hers until I felt the muscles of her thighs twitch under my grip. I kept going, pushing her over the edge and drinking in every sweet sound of pleasure she made.

Then I did it again.

And again.

Standing, I slapped her ass playfully as she twitched and trembled, naked against the unforgiving wood of the desk. Cara turned her head slowly, her hair flopping over the side of her face as she looked at me.

"Can you stand?" I asked, letting the deep seduction ooze through my voice.

Cara shook her head with slow, small movements. "No."

"Good," I growled out, scooping her up and throwing her limp form over my shoulder before heading toward the bedroom. "I'm not finished with you yet."

CHAPTER
17

CARA

Lord, help me.

My legs were jelly by the time Emrick rolled off me hours later, my hands trapped under my body as I lay on my stomach and drew my legs together. Emrick had my ass propped up with a pillow under my hips and had bound my hands before pushing me down onto the bed and crushed me under his weight. He was a dominating force in both physical size and personality, and he excited me more than anyone I had known before. The aura of danger radiated about him, but I knew there was something else to him and could hold hope he'd tell me his secrets soon.

Maybe I would tell him mine.

Emrick slid his cock out of my ass. After using my pussy several times, he wanted to penetrate my ass again before he went to sleep. This time he was mercifully gentle but still managed to bring me to a screaming orgasm as I clenched my fingers, gripping my hands together as my body shook with the power of my release.

He lay on his back, his breathing heavy and loud for a few minutes before it slowed and calmed. I waited, the discomfort settling in when he didn't move after a few more minutes.

"Umm… Emrick?" I whispered. He groaned but didn't say anything. "Can you… uh, untie my hands, please?" I felt his shoulders shake where he lay. "Are you *laughing* at me?" I bristled.

He chuckled again, the mattress depressing as he rolled to face me. "Yeah." He stroked my hair, lifting it away from my face as I lay, hips lifted with my ass on display. "Poor little pussycat, lying there with a sore asshole and tied up, unable to move."

My pussy tingled at his words, and I clenched my legs together. His eyes darkened, and a shadowy smile crept across his face. Before he could speak, I cut him off, "Just let me get a few hours' sleep first, okay?"

"I could fuck you for the rest of the night and into tomorrow night if you let me."

"I don't think I could take it."

His lip lifted into a snarl. "I'll make sure you can."

Licking my lips, I then dragged my teeth across my bottom lip. "Please untie me."

Groaning, he sat up and rolled me over to untie the binds on my wrists. "Stay here," he grunted, rolling off the bed and walking to the bathroom. He came back with a damp hand towel and tossed it at me before returning to the bathroom. I cleaned myself up while listening to the tap running and water splashing. Emrick emerged from the bathroom, wiping down his face with a towel while the loose hair that had come out of his ponytail dripped. Getting up from the bed, I went to the bathroom to clean up before washing my face and rinsing out my mouth. As I clambered back into the bed, he handed me a bottle of water, which I took a grateful swig from.

"Don't think I've ever seen you drink anything other than vodka," I remarked.

He smirked, sipping his water and saying nothing.

Silence fell over us, and the discomfort began to prickle at the back of my neck at how he was looking at me. Putting the lid back on the bottle, I slid under the sheets, pausing to cast Emrick a sideways glance to see if he would tell me to leave, but he had no objections. I pulled the light sheet over my chest, rested my head on my hand, and watched him as he lay down next to me. I allowed myself to get lost in the darkness of his eyes as he stared at me, the loose tendrils of his hair fell about his face.

"Tell me about your darkness," he said, and the creeping feeling returned to the back of my neck.

"W-what do you mean?" I stammered. I wanted to know his story, and, of course, I suspect that would mean he'd want to know mine. But when it came to opening up, I retreated inside.

Because no one knew this side of me, and I don't know what Emrick saw when he looked at me. What if whatever image he had of me was shattered when he found out the truth?

"You said you did some terrible things, that you're messed up. I want you to tell me." When I shifted uncomfortably in the bed, he grabbed my chin, running his thumb across my bottom lip. "Tell me, *everything,*" he growled out the words.

"Fine," I snapped at him. He waited while I stared at him, rolling around several different ways to start this story in my mouth, but none of them felt right.

There was no right way to say such things.

"My father abused me," I spat the words out, letting them tumble into the silence between us. His expression didn't change, and I found myself missing the sunglasses he hid behind—it would be easier to tell this to a blank slate than those dark, analyzing eyes. "There's no nice word for it, he'd rape me, often. There was no one to protect me." I felt my expression darken. "But when he went for my little sister, I knew he had to be stopped."

"You have a sister?"

He was still holding my chin, and I rolled my eyes away from him, blinking away the tears. "I *had* a sister."

There was a shadow of a frown on his face as he continued to stroke my chin, waiting for me to continue. "Is he the reason you don't swear?"

It was my turn to frown, such a fine detail for him to pick up on. "You noticed I don't swear?"

Dropping his hand from my face, he lifted a shoulder in a half-shrug, the gesture at odds with the concern in his eyes. "Place like this, it stands out."

"To everyone?"

His dark eyes flashed. "To me. Keep going."

"He lost interest in me as I got older. I guess fourteen was too old for the sick fuck." His eyebrows shot up when I cursed, and at the shudder that followed the word. "So he went for Angie, and I couldn't let that happen."

It was hard to say these things out loud, harder than I thought it would be. I'd let this part of me build up inside to a dark orb I carried around, and cracking it open felt like I was letting the blackness inside infect my veins.

"He had a gun..." I said quickly. "And I got my hands on it, but..." Emrick waited, and his gorgeous dark eyes watched me, soothing my soul, "... I was young, stupid, and acting on impulse. I could hear her screaming, and I couldn't take it. I *could not* let him do to her what he did to me. She was only eleven... a child."

"You shot him."

"I tried to." I bit my lip so hard I tasted the metallic sting of blood. "I missed." His eyes widened as though he knew what was coming next. "It was so loud, and the kickback from the gun pushed me, and I tripped. When I stood, he was still there, and my sister was... Angie was..."

"Dead."

A shuddering breath escaped. "Yes. I killed her. She was dead because of me."

"It was an accident, Cara."

I shook my head, waving his hand away when he tried to take mine. "I'm not finished." When he looked at me, I frowned. I knew that look, the look said *how much worse can it get?*

"He took it out on me afterward. Somehow he convinced the police it was an accident, I was young and out of my mind, I didn't know what I was doing. Maybe he told them there was an intruder, the details are fuzzy. All I know is I was being sent home with the monster who tore my world apart, and his attacks were worse than before, more violent, as though to make me pay for denying him Angie.

"When I was sixteen, I got a boyfriend, Aiden. He was twenty-two, and he wasn't a good man, but he doted on me, making me feel so good, and when I finally trusted him to touch me, he taught me what it was to make love and to orgasm. He taught me what my father did wasn't sex, it was rape, and sex was different. He also taught me to shoot, and when I finally told him everything, we made a plan to kill my father."

"Understandable."

I raised a brow at Emrick and hummed my acknowledgment. "Yeah, I guess so. So, Aiden came in through the window one night with guns. I told him I wanted the kill shot, he could take out his legs, do whatever, but I wanted to kill him. When I stood over my father with that gun, Emrick, my God, the *power* that surged through me. He begged, *begged!* The nerve. There was no one to save him. No little girl he could push in front of him and use as a human shield. It was between him, me, and the bullet. Aiden stood behind me, egging me on, he was so excited about seeing my father die. I now wonder if he really cared about me or if he just liked watching people die."

"You took the shot."

"Of course, I took the shot! After what he did, he didn't deserve to *live.*" Emrick gave me a moment to take some steadying breaths, and I swiped angrily at my eyes, refusing to let the tears through. "My finger pulled that trigger, the bullet shot out of the gun and pushed through that asshole's skull, killing him instantly. It was merciful, and I wish I had the skill or frame of mind to do something else, maybe his stomach so he bled out or something. I don't know. But faced with him like that, all I felt was anger, and I kept seeing Angie's face. I can't even see her anymore without seeing her blood splattered across my father's chest. I can't even *see* her in my mind anymore, the way she was before the attacks. He died too quickly, and I regret *that.*"

"What happened then?"

My face was void of expression as I faced Emrick. "Aiden fucked me right there in the same room as my father's corpse. He fucked me hard and rough, and I came over and over, and it was the best sex I'd ever had. I rejoiced in it, in the joining of pleasure and pain, physical, mental, and spiritual. Of the blood on my hands and knees as I kneeled, taking him from behind. Of the death of the man who caused all my pain and the penetration and pain which brought me pleasure. It turned me on, and I guess it skewed the lines between sex and violence. I'm not going to use it as an excuse, and I'd never claim everyone who likes it a bit rough is messed up like me, but I *get off* on it in a way I shouldn't. This is my story, this is who I am, and I can't change it." I had been glancing around the room as I talked, but when I looked back at Emrick, he was holding my gaze as though he never looked away the entire time I regaled my sad, sorry tale. "This is why I didn't want to be with you in that way because I knew you would bring the darkness out in me."

"There's nothing wrong with enjoying the power."

I shook my head, letting my hair fall in front of my face to cover my expression, twisted from the pain. "It's the wrong sort of pleasure to feel, for the wrong sort of power. Then I met a man while I was working at The Palace, who exuded this power and aura, and I couldn't resist him. The sex ignited something in me, something I thought I had better control of."

"So, you were never scared of me?"

There was something in his eyes I couldn't place as I answered, "I was, and I wasn't. I was more scared—"

"That I'd bring out this part of you."

"Yeah."

Emrick's expression darkened, and his hand clamped over my arm. "Embrace it."

"What?"

"Embrace the darkness, let it take over you."

"I've spent a decade trying *not* to let it take me over."

"And you've done nothing but struggle. I say embrace it, acknowledge you're darker and different than the rest. Your experiences have made you who you are and shaped you. Take that and run with it. *Let* it shape you, *make* it yours. Don't let the experience make you hide."

"Is that what you do? Embrace the darkness?"

"Yes."

"And how's that working out for you?"

"Fine until you came along and started playing the role of my conscience."

"Innocent people don't deserve to die, Emrick."

"Who are you to decide who's innocent?"

I shrugged. "No one. I'm no one."

"You're someone to me. More worthy than I."

Staring hard at each other, his hand was still gripping my wrist, and I twisted until he let go and allowed me to take his hand. Holding his hand felt strange like it was too simple and intimate of a gesture for us to share. "I think it's time you told me your story, don't you?" I had to grip his hand to stop him from sliding his fingers from mine. "No! Don't you pull away now. I've told you my deepest, darkest secrets. The part of me I've kept locked away for so long, the part of me *you* brought closer to the surface when you took me to bed, the part... what are you smirking about?"

His smirk vanished. "I'm sorry, just *took me to bed* sounds so sweet and innocent considering what we did there."

"What *you* did to *me*, you mean."

His lip twitched. "You loved it."

I couldn't meet his eyes for a moment. He was right. Of course, he was, but I needed to know who this man really was. "Tell me about the scars, Emrick."

CHAPTER
18

EMRICK

She wanted to know about the scars.

The story I could tell her wouldn't be easy because the entire time I'd see Emily's face swimming before me, merging with Cara's, messing with my mind and my sense of reality. But how to explain I fell and what I was before? I couldn't show her my wings, couldn't prove to her I used to be immortal when I no longer was. She'd simply have to trust me and believe something almost all humans would consider completely crazy.

And I wasn't someone to be trusted.

Cara was gripping my hand, whether through support or fear, I wasn't sure. She was right, she had spilled her secrets to me, and it was time for me to return the favor. What's the worst that could happen? Apart from the lingering fear that had been growing in my mind ever since Cara first told me she was thinking of leaving this city. The fear of losing her, which for some inexplicable reason, was something I cared about. She was darkness, I knew her darkness now, and mine recognized hers. Yet somehow, she managed to go through life and not become like me. She wanted the violence and the power it brought, desired it, yet fought against the need for it and tried to be normal.

It would be wrong of me to corrupt her, to try to get her to embrace that side of her, but I was selfish and wanted her for my own, even if it meant breaking down all the walls she had spent so long painstakingly putting together.

"I killed some men," I said finally. "The first men I ever killed."

She was searching my eyes, looking for something beyond the truth. This was nothing she didn't know, nothing everyone in this city didn't already know. There had to be more.

There was, of course.

Sighing, I focused on the feel of her hand in mine, thinking of Emily's. My large hand encased hers, but where I ran my thumb across the inside of her palm, it was different. Where Emily's hands were dry from constant baking and cleaning up the tables and equipment, Cara's hands were smooth and clean. No flour under her nails, which rather than keeping short for practicality, they were long and painted with polish. But not fake, I was pleased to see. Aside from the mask she wore, there was nothing fake about her. Not only did I want her and continued wanting her even after I'd had her, I wanted the *real* Cara.

Emily was my light, bringing out the best in me and showing me the true value of love and humanity and all it had to offer.

Cara was the darkness to mine, and I loved her just the same.

Fuck.

Loved her?

No, I can't. I don't have it in me to love anymore.

"I loved her," I whispered into the silent room, still rubbing Cara's palm. "Emily, she was so beautiful. All she ever wanted in life was a bakery of her own, and when she achieved it, she just *lit up*, like the light was coming from inside her. She'd always greet customers with a smile, but she had a special smile, a brighter one she reserved only for me. Every day I'd go to see her, and I fell in love with her, and she with me."

The light I felt ignite in my chest thinking of Emily was extinguished when the darkness took back over, creeping through my memories and infecting my veins. "But this city is a dark place, full of dark people. I should have taken her away when I had the chance, far from here. But she was so happy, she'd never leave the bakery or her sister and nieces. But the bakery was owned by the insect who used to run this city before me and right next door to one of his clubs. They expected her to pay protection money." A shuddering breath rippled through me, and Cara gripped my hand. "She didn't understand how it worked… she was innocent and naïve. So, they made an example of her."

I made a gun with my fore and middle fingers, holding it up to Cara's face with my thumb raised. "Shot her, point blank in the face, destroying her beauty and taking her soul. I'll never get that image out of my head." Cara's eyes were swimming with tears when I looked at her. "Like you and Angie, I can't even see Emily's face now without seeing how she was when I found her. She left the door unlocked for me… *for me*. Because of *me*, it was so easy for them. She didn't have time to run, and she didn't stand a chance."

"Emrick…" Cara whispered, and I gripped her hand hard enough to make her wince.

"So…" I let the darkness take over my body and voice. "I went for the men who came for her and killed them all. Violently, painfully, marking the street with their blood. I did it even knowing they would take my wings. I didn't care, and I don't regret it."

Cara was frowning. "What do you mean… *take your wings?*"

"It doesn't matter, I don't expect you to believe

me. If I tell you I was an angel and now I'm one of the fallen, you'll never believe me. Those scars on my back are reminders I carry with me every day of the purity I lost, but that part of me was already lost the second that bullet ripped through Emily's skull."

She was processing my words, probably deciding that aligning myself as a fallen angel was some sort of metaphor that helped me deal with the grief. I didn't mind—whatever helped her process it was fine with me. If there were to be something ongoing, then I'd sort the problem of how to prove to her what I was later.

"So, you took over the business?" she asked, apparently deciding to put the fallen angel thing aside for now.

"Not straight away. I went into a dark spiral of despair and anger, and gathered a few followers. Taking the business came a couple of years later, but any qualms or hesitations I may have had with how I forced that transition were crushed the moment I realized this was the same business that owned Emily's bakery, and therefore, the same man who ordered her death. I tried to find him after I had taken over, but he disappeared, exactly as I told him to in order to keep his family safe. Lucky for him, someone else got to him first. His main rival took him down once he was unprotected, so essentially, his death is on me too. But I don't care."

"I don't blame you," Cara mumbled. After a beat where she watched our hands intertwined, she sighed. "So we're both dark people with dark pasts, who secretly…" she raised her brows at me, "… or not-so-secretly enjoy violence and sex. So, where do we go from here?"

"Wherever we want. You say you want to leave this city, but you could make a life here."

"Is that an offer?"

"Depends on your answer."

She smirked. "It's unusual to expect an answer before asking the question."

"I don't like leaving things up to chance."

"So what? I become like a mob wife?"

I barked out a laugh. "Whatever you want to call it. But I think you're more suited to being more involved than that. Although eventually, you'll have to admit we can't be letting everyone go with a second chance. To survive here, to keep this position, some people need to be taken down."

Cara was watching me, and I couldn't read what she was thinking.

CHAPTER 19

CARA

A fallen angel.

It wasn't something I had heard before, but if that's how he needed to identify himself to deal with the pain of Emily's loss, then that was fine with me. There were far greater messed-up people in the world than us, and until Emrick, I had been searching for the same high I got when having sex with Aiden after killing my father, the high that was almost matched with the one-night stand and a new level Emrick elevated me to through the meeting of pleasure and pain.

I was no one to judge him.

Aiden was much too good at covering up what we had done, and I knew he had killed before. He knew the police would never believe I *accidentally* shot my father, after accidentally shooting my sister. It was too much of a coincidence, and any good detective didn't believe in coincidences.

Get rid of the body.

I shook the thoughts from my head. That smell of flesh and bone being devoured by acid was something I could do without remembering.

Emrick's darkness mirrored mine, and although we had taken different paths, we had both ended up here in this bed. He touched me in a way no one else could, unbridled rage and passion burst forth from him when he penetrated me, barely controlling his urges and strength. I loved it and got lost in every moment. I didn't *need* the violence with him, the sex was almost violent enough to cover that desire too.

In some messed-up way, this man was what I needed.

So did I still need to flee this city? Should I run from the memories this place held? Or should I do as Emrick does and embrace it? Let the darkness be my power, and then no one can mess with me. What were my goals in life anyway? Was I after a husband and kids? It didn't feel right. I wanted to get away but had no plans after that. Maybe my messed-up self would seek out some sort of darkness in another city, and I was doomed to repeat the past.

But here, with him, I had everything I needed and wanted.

Leaning forward, I kissed him, our fingers still clasped together between us. Keeping it chaste, I then pulled away, watching his eyes for an answer or anything to tell me what he was thinking. But he dropped my hand and wound his fingers through my hair, yanking my face to his and crashing his lips on mine. He was forceful immediately, pushing his tongue into my mouth and swallowing my moans when he used his other hand to grasp my breast, flicking and pinching the nipple between his fingers.

He rolled over on top of me, pushing and shifting my body, small under his until I was sitting upright against the headboard. I opened my mouth to ask what he was doing, and he stuck three fingers on my tongue, groaning when I sucked his fingers.

"That's it," he growled out. "That's what I need from you."

Kneeling in front of me, he grabbed my head and guided my mouth onto his already erect cock, pushing in until he was almost against the back of my throat. Breathing through my nose, I worked to calm my gag reflex, the movement making my tongue massage the sensitive skin on the underside of his cock, pulling a moan from him. Looking down at me, Emrick placed his hands on the wall and began fucking my mouth. When I went to touch him, he slapped my hands away.

"Keep those hands to yourself, pussycat." He panted. "Let me fuck that pretty mouth of yours."

Groaning around him as he forced his length in

and out of my mouth, my pussy tingled, already wet and waiting for him. Pulling back, he gave me a moment to cough and swallow the spit before pushing back in, chuckling through his moans and keeping his eyes on mine. His balls tightened, and I prepared myself to swallow his load when the bedroom door slammed open.

Ripping his cock from my mouth, he spun, shielding my body with his from the gun that was pointed directly at us.

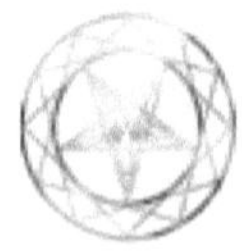

"Oh, put some fucking clothes on. I don't want to look at your cock."

Emrick shrugged, unabashed with his nudity, his cock still hard and dripping with my spit despite the danger we were in. Reaching a hand behind him, he made a hidden gesture at me. I had no idea what it meant and didn't have time to think before he moved slowly off the bed to find his pants.

Maddie stood in the doorway, a gun pointed directly at Emrick as he moved around the room before stopping to get dressed. Behind her with his arms crossed over his chest was Tate.

Emrick moved to stand at the end of the bed,

linking his hands behind his back and making the same gesture at me.

"I knew you two were involved somehow," Maddie said. "I *warned* you, Cara. I tried to get you to stay away from him. I knew he was going down. Now you're dating or some shit. You're literally in bed with the enemy!"

"You're the one with the gun, Maddie. From where I'm sitting, you're the enemy right now."

"We're not *dating*," Emrick hissed.

Maddie ignored me, cocking a brow at Emrick. "Oh?" The gun's barrel swerved toward me, and she cocked it, her finger twitching on the trigger. "Then you won't mind if I kill her?"

"No!" Emrick roared, holding a hand out and taking a half step forward.

Maddie returned the gun's aim to him and smirked. "Oooh," she drew out the word, heavy with sarcasm and victory. "So you *do* care what happens to her."

The look in her eyes shook me because I knew that look. If she had to shoot me then and there to prove a point to Emrick, then she would have. There was *intent* behind her eyes, intent to follow through and take my life. After everything, after how long we have known each other, she had been right— when it came down to it, she'd choose herself over me any day. I was as expendable as anyone else in this city to her. I was nothing. There wasn't an ounce of remorse on her face.

I was yanked from my shock when my eyes were drawn to the movement of Emrick's hands behind his back. There was that gesture again. Desperately I tried to figure out what he wanted me to do as he confronted Tate.

"I should've known you were behind this," Emrick said coolly.

"Should've but didn't." Tate seemed unconcerned with the situation, his tight black T-shirt clinging to his muscles as he stood casually slightly behind Maddie, who held a triumphant grin on her face. "You were sloppy, Emrick, you didn't know shit about running a business like this. Loyalty doesn't mean spit. You need to get resources, and always... *always* do a background check on your employees because you never know who you have working for you."

"And who did I have working for me?"

"In a previous life, I was Thomas Murphy. If you weren't so fucking arrogant and had done even an iota of research, you would have known who I was from day one."

Emrick stared at him without speaking, then a muscle in his neck twitched. "Murphy."

"Yeah, the fucker you threatened and kicked out of here was my father. This business should've been mine. Did you know he died shortly after what you did? He left here to protect his family, his daughter more than me, and then without the protection of the club and his business, his biggest rival came for him." Tate scoffed. "But I bet you don't care."

Shrugging, Emrick's voice was still cool. "You're right, I don't care. He took what meant most to me, so I have no regrets over his death. If I had known who he was before I shafted him out, I'd have killed him myself. So, the man who took his life did me a favor."

Tate smirked, and his demeanor changed. "Turns out, they did me a favor too. Murphy had cut me out of the business, and I was getting ready to fight my way back in. After all he had put me through, the fucker thought he could just cut me out. Then you came along and swept the business out from under him, and my opportunity to get back in arose."

"Why not kill me, Tate?"

"You were good at one thing, Emrick... building the empire. So, I let you. I let you do all the hard work for me. Then all I needed to do was destroy the business' trust in *you*, and it wasn't difficult to make you look incapable. The loss of a few inconsequential buildings was nothing compared to the loss of trust that was growing in your ability to run this business. Employees can be turned with money too easily when they feel the boss can no longer protect them. It was easy to make you look weak because you are. Your celestial strength and remaining invulnerability doesn't make you smart."

My head snapped up.

Celestial strength? Surely, Tate didn't buy into this whole fallen angel thing.

But then Tate's eyes turned yellow.

What the fuck?

Maddie didn't see Tate's eyes. She was staring firmly at Emrick, and he tilted his head at her. "And what's your stake in this, whore?"

Maddie lifted a shoulder. "Money, lots of money." As I reached over the side of the bed, Maddie screamed at me, "Stay still!"

"I'm just getting a T-shirt," I said, holding up the gray shirt I had seen on the floor. Maddie's stance relaxed slightly as I pulled the T-shirt on, but when I had leaned over, I'd seen it, what Emrick had been trying to signal to me.

A gun under the pillow.

Of course, he slept with a gun under his pillow.

Lifting the pillow and holding it against the front of me, hoping it looked like I was trying to cover my body, the T-shirt not quite covering my thighs, I hid the gun between the pillow and my body and slowly moved off the bed to stand next to Emrick.

"Why are you doing this, Maddie?" I asked.

"I already told you, *money.*"

"Maddie, you promised, you *promised* you would leave. Emrick spared your life and you *promised.* I defended you, you're only alive because of me!"

"I still don't understand how you can be so naïve,

Cara." Maddie shook her head. "Promises and loyalty mean nothing here."

"And friendship?"

She stared hard at me. "Everyone for themselves."

"Are you going to kill me, Maddie?"

"Not you, not unless you make me. Only him."

"And you could do that? After how long we've known each other? You could kill me?" I hissed at her.

"Don't try me. You think you're protected just because you're fucking the boss? You chose the wrong side."

My eyes darted between the gun in Maddie's hand as she cocked it, and Emrick, who didn't take his eyes off Maddie. I had to stop her, so I changed my tone again, trying to keep the attitude to a minimum, although what I wanted to do was beat the crap out of her. "Maddie, please don't do this. It's not too late to leave now."

"Tate takes over the business, and I get to have whatever I want."

"Why is he making you do his dirty work like a coward?"

Tate snarled at me but said nothing.

Maddie laughed. "Call it an initiation." When her finger found the trigger, something switched inside me. My eyes darkened, and for a second, Maddie's gaze was torn from Emrick and fell on me.

The gun was so heavy in my hands, I wasn't prepared for how heavy it was. He was on top of Angie, and I couldn't take her screams. They echoed in my mind and would torture me forever. The sick pig could do what he pleased with me, but I let him because I thought that meant he'd leave Angie alone. When he went for her, I couldn't take it, and I would not let him destroy her as he had me.

"Stop!" He turned at my cry, rolling over onto his back and pulling Angie with him. She stared at the gun in my shaking hands, tears streaming down her cheeks to match my own. "Leave her alone."

"Get out of here, Cara. I'll be in to see you later."

My stomach churned and legs weakened, but I tightened my grip on the gun. The monster's eyes widened when I cocked the gun. I'd never shot anything before, but I'd seen movies.

It seemed fairly simple, point and shoot, and the bad guy would be dead.

I could see his head and aimed with my eyes narrowed, lining it up as best I could.

My fingers pulled the trigger.

If there was one thing I learned...

"Never close your eyes when you pull the trigger," I whispered to myself.

Eyeing Maddie, I raised my voice, "I'd tell you not

to do it because killing someone changes who you are." I kept my voice even through no feat of willpower because I no longer felt threatened by her. She was the weak one. "But the truth is, I simply don't think you have it in you."

The shot rang out a fraction of a second before Maddie collapsed to the floor. My aim was true this time. After years of secret practice, I promised I'd never miss again. I had no plans to ever raise a gun to another human, but when I was facing the practice target on the range, the power of the weapon surged through my fingers, and I saw his face.

Every time.

Never close your eyes when you pull the trigger.

There was enough control in me not to aim for her face, but a shot to the throat took her out just as fast—a merciful kill. I dropped the pillow, cocking the gun again and turning it on Tate. I understood the rules of this city and knew it was everyone for themselves. But to pull a gun on someone, simply to prove you were worthy of dirty money, screw that.

Especially to pull a gun on Emrick.

Because he was mine as much as I was his. I cared more she had threatened his life than she had threatened mine.

It's a flimsy line to walk, and yes, I killed someone over it, over him.

But I never claimed to be one of the good guys.

Embrace the darkness.

Tate glanced uninterested in the gun and launched himself over Maddie's body at Emrick. I fired, an explosion of red ripped from his shoulder as the bullet hit his back. But he didn't stop, and Tate and Emrick fell together, wrestling with each other on the carpet.

Tate managed to get hold of Emrick and threw him into the wall. I screamed as the wall caved in where he landed, the plaster and brick crumbling over him as he hit the floor. Firing another shot at Tate, this one went through his leg, but he still didn't stop. He stormed over to me, snatching the gun from my hand and released the clip before tossing it across the room. With a backhanded slap that held more strength than I was prepared for, I hit the floor. Sitting up, I shuffled backward away from the fight as Emrick and Tate collided again, two unstoppable forces meeting. Each punch was delivered with the intent to get the upper hand in order to kill, and Emrick's face was a bloody mess that matched Tate's within minutes.

Searching desperately around the room with my eyes for something I could use to help, I grabbed a bottle of vodka from the bedside table. Breaking it over Tate's head, he roared in rage, turning and shoving me away from him, knocking me off my feet again.

Emrick's face darkened, and he growled at Tate,

picking him up and holding him over his head. With three struggling steps trying to keep hold of Tate's body, twisting in his grip, Emrick moved toward the window.

The window shattered, the wooden frame splintering as Emrick threw Tate through the glass. Pushing myself to my feet, I rushed across the room, coming up next to Emrick as he collapsed to his knees. Leaning out the window, I withdrew my hand sharply, cradling it against my chest after I cut myself on a shard of glass before looking down to the street.

Three stories.

The fall wouldn't kill him, but it should certainly injure him enough to incapacitate him for a while.

Yet when I looked, he was pushing himself to his feet, his movement not appearing hindered by any injury. Tate stared up at me, those yellow eyes blazing in the night as onlookers backed away from him.

Spitting at the entrance to the building, Tate shoved his hands in his pockets and walked away, disappearing into the night.

Kneeling next to Emrick, I cradled his face in my hands, assessing his injuries.

"Are you okay?"

In response, Emrick spat a mouthful of blood onto the carpet. "I will be. Tate?"

I shook my head. "He left." Glancing up at the

blanket of the night sky out the window, I turned back to Emrick. "It's not over, is it?"

Emrick tilted his head toward the window. "No, it's not over. He'll come back." With a grunt, he heaved himself to his feet, and I hated the blood that caked his face. I wanted to kill Tate for what he had done, so I couldn't imagine the rage that Emrick was feeling, but he kept his expression impassive and stared out the broken window. "And I'll be ready for him when he does."

CHAPTER
20

EMRICK

She was a natural.

Cara had embraced the darkness, and she was incredible.

The clean-up crew came in and got rid of Maddie's body. A shot to the neck, I hadn't expected that. I thought Maddie and Cara were close, but apparently Maddie had motivations that were shallower than Cara had hoped of her. Foolish, and I wondered where this persistent part of her that always tried to see the best in people came from. Human nature, perhaps. I thought I'd need to comfort Cara after the death of her friend, but instead, I found a new layer of darkness in her eyes.

Should I feel guilty for being the one to bring it out in her? She had spent so long trying to keep it down, but she was embracing it now because of me.

So I felt no guilt.

Hell, before the crew even came in, she had dragged me into the bathroom, and we fucked in the shower, *hard*. My blood from my injuries, still slower to heal than they used to be, washed over our bodies as I took her. I ignored the pain, embraced it, as my body objected to being put to use so soon after the fight. I still lifted her against the cold tiles and sunk my cock into her tight cunt. She took everything I had to give and more, and the shower was able to wash away the additional blood after I bit into her neck.

She was almost perfect.

Now I only needed to get her used to me fucking her ass as hard as I did her little cunt.

Then she'd be perfect.

There were already cops under my payroll. Of course, there had to be to look the other way. But I needed more. Cara pushed me to pay a few bribes to get some of them on my good side, and thanks to Tate's suggestion, I used the police resources to conduct background checks on all my employees.

Only three people needed to be fired due to previous connections to the Murphy family—no loss. Even if they had no intention of doing anything, after Tate, I couldn't take another risk. Cara shot one of them in the foot when they started getting angry about it.

Damn, she was really embracing this shit. It was

like a light switch had been flicked inside her, and the moment she decided she was no longer going to fight this part of herself, she just morphed into this twisted woman. How she even hid it for as long as she did, I had no idea. She was the sort of person I'd have tried to help in the old days as a Watcher, but those days were gone, and I liked her how she was, fucked-up tendencies and all.

Despite Tate's betrayal only increasing my distrust in demons, the demons that were on the payroll, I kept on board. *Better the devil you know* and all of that *keep your enemies close.* Besides, they were fairly low on the food chain—grunt workers, muscle—paid to do all the shit I didn't want to deal with but they enjoyed. They came and went as they pleased between Hell and Earth, and I didn't care as long as they were there when I needed them, and they kept coming back because I provided them with an outlet for their demonic desires.

Tate was correct—I had taken over this business in a fit of rage and made most things up as I went along. There were a lot of holes in my business plan, some of them had been exploited already, and others were open for the taking. But not anymore. I employed Sven to step up and use his previous experience—things that came up in the background check, a history in security services before he was caught using the company information to rob and kill—to find potential security issues and fix them.

Tate had helped me more by attempting to bring me down than he had directly over the years he was with me.

He should have killed me rather than attempting to destroy trust in me.

Fucking prick.

Whatever, while I knew he'd be back, I'd deal with him when that time came around. Or perhaps I'd seek him out myself, get to him before he had a chance to rally too much support. There was no shortage of enemies out there who would move against me given the chance. But for now, we were busy claiming insurance on the destroyed buildings, rebuilding those I wanted to save, and reworking any issues that could lead to another attempt to bring me down. All of this took longer than it should have. Of course, the buildings weren't directly in my name, that would be foolish, but they were twisted up in entities and trusts.

Tate had offered me a valuable commodity—time to fix my mistakes.

I couldn't help but wonder what he was doing with this time in return before he came back to finish our unsettled business.

Cara still wanted to work the floor because she said that sitting around while I took care of business wasn't her style.

"Cara!"

My knuckles gripped the bar on the balcony as I leaned over the edge, my eyes sweeping the floor behind the dark sunglasses. Some asshole had just tried to slide a tip into the side of her skirt, and to save myself from ripping his arms from his body, I needed to get her to come to me.

Besides, I had a visitor I needed her to meet.

"You don't need to yell at her like that," Zaqiel said calmly.

"Fuck off, she's mine. I can talk to her how I want."

His face darkened. "You can't *own* a person, Emrick."

Cara appeared at the doorway at the top of the stairs, and I stormed over to her, grabbing the front of her skirt and yanking her to me. Kissing my way up her neck before devouring her mouth, I pulled away from the kiss and finished by tugging on her bottom lip with my teeth. She stood there with her eyes closed and head tilted up toward me.

"Who owns you, pussycat?" I asked.

"You do," she whispered.

Turning back to Zaqiel, I smirked as he rolled his eyes, turning away from the display. Grabbing Cara's arm, I steered her toward the couch. "I have someone for you to meet." Indicating to Zaqiel, who stood and shook Cara's hand, I said, "This is Zaqiel, my brother, who still hasn't told me why he's here after over ten fucking years."

Cara's brows shot up. "Well, that's… quite the introduction."

Zaqiel pressed his lips together. "Sorry about that." He turned to me as Cara poured herself a glass of whiskey, taking a seat on the couch next to Zaqiel as I sat in my regular chair and slid my sunglasses off. Leaning my elbows on my knees, I stared hard at Zaqiel, taking him in. He looked the same. Same short hair and built form, now slightly leaner than me as I had worked hard on bulking myself up further to increase the intimidation factor.

"Why are you here?"

After taking a sip of his drink, he placed it on the glass table, leaning back on the couch and crossing an ankle over his other knee. "A long time ago, you told me one day I'd understand…" He cleared his throat, casting a glance at Cara who simply raised her brows at him again. "That I would understand what it felt like to want to kill a human."

My eyes widened, and I leaned forward in my chair. "Did you kill someone?"

He looked as though I had slapped him. "No, of course not." But his hand trembled when he took another drink. "But maybe, I uh… set something in motion…"

"Oh, brother," I cried out, clapping, the delight flooding through me. Earth had corrupted Zaqiel, of all the angels, it was uptight and upright Zaqiel. But my elation was short-lived as all the emotions I had experienced when we last saw each other came back, overtaking the moment where there was a brief glimpse of how we used to be. I could almost feel the rain on my shoulders as I looked into his deep blue eyes, seeing the judgment there and knowing I was about to lose my wings by taking revenge for the woman I loved. I was on the edge of losing everything because the one thing I loved most in the world had already been taken from me.

Zaqiel and I stared at each other and for a long while Cara kept quiet simply watching us. There was so much I wanted to say to him. I wanted to be angry, to blame him for my falling. I wanted to scream at him, to take his throat in my hands and bang his head on the floor, and hope he felt some semblance of the pain I had endured.

But he had changed. I could see it in his eyes. Did he love someone too? A human? Had he had someone killed to protect them? There was nothing in the air between us I could sense that indicated he was fallen, so either he had been extraordinarily careful about setting the human up to die, or he was destined to die. More of this predetermination shit.

Or God simply loved him more than he loved me. I doubted even He was above showing favoritism.

There was something I needed to do more than shout at Zaqiel, and although a muscle twitched in my neck at the thought, there was a greater ache in my chest, a hole that needed to be healed.

I'd deny it, though, and would kill anyone who asked.

Standing abruptly, Zaqiel's gaze followed my movement, and he stood too, a moment later, slowly and steadily drawing himself to his full height until we were eye to eye. Part of me wanted to punch his perfect face, and I wondered if I'd be fast enough to get one in before he stopped me. He still had his full celestial strength and speed, mine was waning with every passing year. Cara was watching us, sipping her drink as though a movie was playing out in front of her, her eyes shifting between us, as curious as to who would make the first move as I was. I wanted to look at her, to remind myself that I had her when before I had nothing. I didn't forgive, and I didn't forget.

But Zaqiel had changed, maybe only a little bit, but perhaps he really had learned something.

"You told me," Zaqiel said, "on that day, we could be brothers again."

"A lot has changed, Zaqiel. I'm a different being now." I tossed a glance at Cara. "I've embraced the anger and hatred, and I've done some terrible, terrible things."

"I know. But I don't blame you."

"Why?"

"Let's just say I've learned a lot myself over the years. I've been meaning to come see you for many months now. I'm sorry it's taken me so long." He sighed again. "I'm not saying we're suddenly going to be best friends or that we can go back to how it was before." I scoffed, and he glared at me. Zaqiel knew as well as I that we were always quite different, even before I fell. He continued, "But I feel that we need to..." clearing his throat, he rubbed the back of his neck before he stretched out his hand between us, "... mend broken bridges."

I stared at his outstretched hand and again wondered what he had been through that had brought him to me. Who had he wanted to kill and why? These are things I'd be asking him, but later. Because there were two things I needed from him first.

One, was something that didn't come naturally to me.

Taking his outstretched hand, I yanked him forward and hugged him.

Almost a hug. It was more a colliding of our shoulders before I pulled away as Zaqiel stiffened.

"That's enough," I said.

"It's good to see you... brother."

Nodding, I stepped away and moved to open the office door. "Before you tell me your entire story and who the unlucky human was who earned your wrath, I need something from you. Step into my office."

He arched an eyebrow before striding past me and into the office. Cara was still silent, and I cleared my throat so she'd look at me. "You too, pussycat. You need to see this."

"All right." As she walked past me, I slapped her ass hard, and she cried out drawing the attention of Zaqiel. He cleared his throat and looked away as I followed her into the office, nipping and kissing at her neck with both hands grabbing at her ass.

"Uh, I'm not sure what you want—" Zaqiel started.

"Oh, grow up. We're not going to have an orgy or anything."

Cara chuckled and leaned against the edge of the desk, crossing her arms and staring at Zaqiel and me in the center of the room. "What's this about?" she asked.

"I was wondering that myself."

I ignored Zaqiel and turned to Cara, her smirk dropping at the look on my face. It was time she knew the truth. "When I told you I was a fallen angel, I know you didn't believe me."

"Oh, Emrick, I—"

She quieted when I held up a hand. "It's the truth, Cara. I was an angel, and now I'm fallen." I glanced at the recently repaired window. "And Tate was infected with demon blood." She raised her brows, and I returned the look. "You shot him twice, Cara, and he didn't even slow down. Didn't that make you wonder?"

"I—"

"And the scars on my back look literally like I had wings cut off."

"There are a lot of things that could've caused those scars," she countered.

"Such as?"

"Um… burns?" she offered weakly.

"I need you to see the truth, and Zaqiel…" I turned to him, "… this is where you come in."

"Emrick, this may not be a good idea. What if she freaks out?"

I had considered this, but if she was going to be my woman, I couldn't have her not knowing the biggest truth about who and what I was. If this meant she ran, left the city as she had planned to all along, and didn't come back, then I'd just have to deal with that.

I'd been alone before, and I could do it again. Even if it cut me up until there was nothing left of me.

She deserved to know.

"Show her, Zaqiel."

He shrugged, and for a moment his indifference to my request struck me. Zaqiel didn't do things without overthinking. Steady Zaqiel, stern and reliable. But he straightened his already squared posture, and with a twitch of his shoulders, he unfurled his wings. Dappled steel and gun-barrel grays, they spread across the office. There was a *clunk* as Cara dropped the glass she'd been holding, her hand remaining in front of her as though she was still clasping it, stiff and unmoving. I moved to her side, glad she was leaning on the desk as she swayed slightly and slid my arm around her waist to take her weight while she sunk down. Her eyes were wide and pupils pinpoints as her gaze swept over Zaqiel's wings. He was watching her face with concern, the muscles in his arms twitching.

Seeing his wings stirred something in me, and the scars on my back tingled with the memory of that lost part of me. I felt naked and exposed at the reminder, and it sent a chill down my spine. When I looked back at Zaqiel, his eyes were on mine, blue on black, and I'm sure he knew exactly what I was thinking. I hadn't been confronted with the loss of my wings so vividly since I last saw him, and I hadn't realized how much it would hurt. They were more than wings, more than a physical limb or presence. They were as much a part of me as my mind, heart, and soul. Without them, I was less than angel, less than human, and the anger flickered in my stomach, reminding me to reclaim the darkness that lived within me. Without apology.

For Emily. For Cara.

My attention was drawn back to Cara when she

started whimpering, her mouth opened and closed as though she wanted to say something but couldn't find the words. I gripped her chin and forced her to look at me. "My wings were taken when I killed those men for killing Emily. This is real, Cara."

She shook her head slowly and tore her gaze from me, returning it to Zaqiel in time to see him fold his wings away until they disappeared from sight. "I'm sorry, Cara," Zaqiel said, "I know this is confronting and can't be easy to accept, but Emrick is telling the truth."

"I can't... I can't deal with this right now," she whispered. I tried to keep my arm around her waist, but she pushed away from the desk, placing a palm on my chest and stepping away from me. "I need..." she glanced at Zaqiel again, shaking her head, "... I need some time."

Without another word, she shoved away from me. I could have held onto her, I'm stronger than she is, and I could have forced her to stay, tying her to the bed and keeping her as my own. The darkness flared inside me at the injustice. I thought of Ray and her bonded partner, a partner who accepted her even though she knew Ray was a demon. Yet this woman I loved, my second chance at life in this world, walked away from me when faced with the truth.

The door closed behind her, and Zaqiel stared at me while I tried to avoid his eye contact, clenching and releasing my fists at my side.

"I'm sorry, Emrick—"

"Don't. Don't be. It was the right thing." I turned to him. "Thanks for coming back, and thank you for helping with Cara. I'll see you later."

"Emrick—"

"Goodbye, Zaqiel."

He nodded stiffly before leaving without another word.

CHAPTER
21

EMRICK

Three days.

She'd been gone three days, and all it made me wish was that she had left like all the others after the night we first fucked. Because this was worse. I had allowed myself to get attached to her. I had discovered who she was beyond the veil she pulled over her inner darkness, and I loved her for it.

We were two beings, embracing the dark side of ourselves without apology. Zaqiel and my other brothers and sisters may not approve, Zaqiel may even be the only other angel I'd ever see again, but none of that mattered. It was fucked up, but I had forged a life here, and along with the power, there was someone by my side I could share it with.

I *had* someone.

She was gone now, and with each passing hour, I

suspected she may not be coming back.

So, I threw myself into work, possibly with more ruthlessness than was required. When the bar manager questioned both Maddie and Cara missing on the same night, joking they were out together trying to pick up, I struck him with my fist.

Then fired him as he lay on the floor.

He looked up at me with those pathetic eyes, blood dripping from his nose, and scampered out of the building without another question. Sven raised a brow at me before shrugging and moving off to begin the search for a replacement. The waitresses steered clear of me, not used to seeing me on the floor, and possibly rightfully guessing I was looking for someone or something to take my anger out on.

Slamming the door behind me as I stepped back onto the balcony, I threw my sunglasses to the side.

"So much drama."

I had drawn and cocked my gun before my mind had registered the voice but kept the weapon pointed at my unexpected visitor to prove a point. "What are you doing here?"

Zaqiel lifted a shoulder. "We're family."

"We used to be."

He arched an eyebrow. "I thought we had a moment."

I scoffed. "We mended a bridge, but we're too different to be dropping in on each other."

"You can't drop in, you don't even know

where I live."

"I don't care."

"That's rude."

"What are you doing here?" I repeated.

"I have a surprise for you." Standing, he moved into my office, and I followed him, jiggling the door handle as I walked past. The lock had been busted, the handle bent and twisted. I glared at Zaqiel, and he simply smiled at me.

"You know you could have just come and got me?"

"Yeah, but this way is more fun."

"Since when have you cared about fun?" I muttered, storming past Zaqiel and shoving him with my shoulder. There was still rage pushing its way through my veins. Having and losing Cara had burned a hole in me and released more anger than I thought I was capable of feeling. She was right, I used anger to cover the pain, and now there was so much more, I'd need to release more fury to cover it.

"This is Evie." Zaqiel indicated to the woman leaning on my desk. Statuesque with long blonde hair that flowed down her back, she was textbook beautiful, but her arms were littered with a crisscross of varying scars. She looked like she had been through Hell and back, and the last thing she needed was the likes of me.

"Please tell me you're not trying to set me up." I

pushed the words through gritted teeth. If this is what he thought was the best way to make up for Emily and Cara…

Zaqiel growled, and my eyebrows shot up. "You don't *touch* her." He snarled at me. I held my hands up, my anger dissipating with the shock of Zaqiel actually *growling* at me. He straightened his shoulders after shaking the tension out, and Evie smiled at him with such endearment I felt the bubble of rage in me again. "Evie is my…" He looked at her with the same expression she gazed at him. "She's *my* Evie, and I got her to talk to Cara."

"About what?"

"About the truth of what we are and coming to accept that."

"She's really sweet, Emrick. You're a lucky man," Evie said, but it sounded scripted.

My lip twitched, and I almost laughed. Yep, she's really sweet, all right. My pussycat who enjoys the mixture of sex and violence and has killed more than one person. She's a doll.

Something about the way Evie was looking at me was off. Her smile was slightly strained, except for those moments when she looked at Zaqiel, then a light would cross over her face, and her expression would soften, making her already attractive features even more beautiful.

I'm sure she knew exactly the sort of man I was and who I was to this city. Perhaps she hated men like me. I eyed her scars again. Perhaps she had justifiably good reason to hate men like me. She was only here as a favor to Zaqiel, that much was abundantly clear.

"So?" I scoffed out.

"So, she wanted some more time to think, but she's certainly feeling better about it, now that the shock has worn off." Evie lifted her shoulder. "And I guess it helps to know she's not the only one struggling with this. I told her my whole story..." she glanced fondly at Zaqiel, "... about how we met, how I found out the truth, and my process of dealing with that. I continued to need to deal with it even after we decided to be together. It was no small feat."

"I feared the truth would break Evie more than once, but she's an incredibly strong woman," Zaqiel added.

"It may have broken me had it not been for the fact I already loved you before I knew you weren't human." Evie turned back to me. "Cara will go through her own journey, as this is a lot to take on. But she's strong, and she loves you. I think she'll come out the other side and come back to you."

My dark eyes shifted out of focus. "She told you she loved me?"

Evie's smile was understanding, and her eyes kind at the talk of love, even though there was still hardness behind her look when she turned to me.

Evie may have been as strong as Zaqiel claimed, but she looked pure enough to be an angel herself, save for the scars. Although we would scar too if we could, given everything our hearts endured. "She didn't have to," Evie said simply.

"Why couldn't you have just called the club and told me this?" I asked.

"I don't have a phone," Zaqiel answered.

"Of course you don't," I muttered before sighing heavily. He'd been trying to fix things, and I couldn't blame him for that. But I wasn't sure if I was relieved about the flicker of hope he had given me or if it only made it worse if Cara ultimately decided not to come back to me.

As the days dragged on, I got worse. I could feel it happening, and I knew my men could see it too. But there was no willpower in me to stop it. I had told Cara to embrace her darkness, and I was embracing mine, letting it fill me up and take me over, allowing it to stamp out that flicker of hope that had foolishly arisen after the visit from Zaqiel and Evie.

I was tempted to find a woman, lure her back to my bedroom, and take out my anger on her, but it would feel empty. All I could do was hope these feelings didn't last for too long, and soon I'd be able to sink my cock into some slut and chase the ultimate high, knowing that it would be enough to burn away my pain for a little while.

My feet were up on the large desk, and I was staring blankly at the glass of vodka in my hand when there was a knock at the door. I grunted, and it swung open, Sven looking around the corner.

"Those drinks you ordered are here, sir."

"I didn't order any fucking drinks."

But he had already disappeared, and when I looked up again, she was closing the door behind her as she carried a tray with a new bottle of vodka and two glasses.

Cara.

She stood uncomfortably while I stared her down, unsure if I wanted to scream at her or embrace her.

Or choke her out.

"Hey," she said finally, and after hesitating a moment longer, she approached the desk, placed the tray down, and poured herself a drink upon seeing I already had one.

"Hey."

My lip twitched as she fidgeted slightly, her thighs rubbed together under her too-short skirt. Tilting my head forward, I surveyed her under my brows, hoping that the blackness of my eyes made her second-guess her decision to be here. I wanted her with me, but I didn't want her to know that, not straight away. I needed her to feel at least a hint of the pain and uncertainty that had plagued me while she had been gone.

Cara took a swig of her drink, which seemed to steady something within her, and she sauntered over to me, sitting on the edge of the desk. My gaze immediately dropped to where her skirt rode up her thigh. Cara's fingers dipped down and pulled her skirt up further as she lifted a leg and placed her foot on my chair between my thighs.

"What are you doing?" my voice was dark and hoarse as I tried and failed to contain emotions I'd never admit to having. My fingers twitched with the urge to touch her and make her hurt. Her toes curled in my crotch, and I felt my cock grow hard. It would be so easy to take her.

"I've had a lot of time to think, and I'm trying to tell you I still want you."

"Why?"

"Because you accept my darkness, and I want to accept yours, even if I don't fully understand it yet."

I walked my fingers up her thigh, sliding under the hem of her skirt, leaving a trail of goose bumps where I touched her. "Do you want to talk about it?" I offered, gritting my teeth to keep myself from taking her right here. Because I didn't want to talk, not now, maybe not ever. Although I knew she'd want to, I would deal with that when it came. Cara had walked willingly back into my office and into my life, and I was about to stake my claim on her for good. Talking could wait because I couldn't hold out that long.

"Not really," she said, shuddering as I slid my fingers further under her skirt. "Not now."

"Good," I growled out.

Grabbing her legs, I yanked her off the edge of the desk, dropping my drink to the floor and knocking hers from her hand ignoring the sound of shattering glass as I made her straddle me. She moaned as I kissed her, forcing her lips open and invading her mouth with my tongue.

"Emrick," she panted as I moved my way down, kissing and nipping at her neck. "There's a lot I still don't understand, and it might take time for me to get my head around it."

She yelped as I pulled the strap of her dress off her shoulder and bit into her creamy skin. She tasted so good. I wanted to make her sweat. I wanted her skin to be salty sweet when I licked it. I wanted droplets of her blood in my mouth as she screamed in pain and pleasure.

She started to talk again, and I slapped a palm over her mouth before moving to slide my fingers into her mouth, feeling her tongue work around them. "I thought you didn't want to talk about it."

"I don't, I just—"

I swallowed her next words with another kiss, and she groaned against my lips as my thumbs dug into the flesh of her thighs, my fingers working their way toward her hot core.

"Shut the fuck up then," I whispered, sliding her panties to the side and feeling her wetness, "... and let me claim you."

She whimpered as I pushed two fingers into her pussy, already wet and waiting for me. When she tried to grind against my hand, I slapped her thigh, making her jump and feeling the surge of power at the way her skin changed hue. I wanted her to hurt because even after she knew my story, she still left me to wallow in the emptiness of her absence, not knowing if she'd come back.

Masking pain with anger was second nature to me now.

With a growl rumbling through my chest, I lifted her off my lap and dropped her onto the desk in front of me, sliding the chair forward so I was seated between her spread thighs. Her scent was intoxicating, marked by my celestial pheromones, sending another growl rumbling through me. A thought pushed its way into my mind, a hope that one of the men or women I had fucked crossed paths with the demon who had slept with Cara, and he could smell me on them, and he knew my power and was threatened by it.

But not Cara, she was mine now, and no other

hands would touch her ever again.

I *owned* her.

Leaning forward, I sunk my teeth into her thigh, holding her when she tried to move away from the assault and marking her again as mine.

Mine.

In my mind, I saw her face, Emily's, in a way I hadn't remembered it in a long time. I remembered how she looked before she was shot before they destroyed her beauty and took her soul. She smiled at me, blew me a kiss, and turned and walked away, disappearing into a part of my mind where she'd always be treasured.

But making room in my heart for Cara.

I couldn't take away the darkness within me, and as sick as it may be, I didn't want to. Because I liked this lifestyle, and I craved the power that came with it, and Cara, she was the perfect one to have by my side. Almost as dark as me, but with a soul left to steer me away from destroying what was left of mine.

Swiping my tongue up her pussy, she shuddered, moaning when I reached her clit and sucked. She grabbed at my head, pulling hair loose from my ponytail, trying to pull me closer to her, desperate for my tongue.

"Touch yourself," I commanded. Leaning back in my chair, I started unbuckling my pants. "Play with that cunt for me."

"Emrick, *please*—"

"If you needed me so badly, you shouldn't have left." Her eyes pleaded with mine, and when she huffed like an insolent teenager, I slapped her thigh again. "None of your attitude, pussycat. You're lucky I haven't shoved my cock into that tight ass of yours without mercy. Now, play with your pussy like a good girl, and maybe I'll fuck you until you come."

Cara shuddered, and I felt the darkness and lust for power surge within me. It was a part of me I thought I was better without but realized I should be taking the advice I gave Cara for myself.

Embrace the darkness.

Her hands wandered between her legs, and she pressed a forefinger to the bud of her clit, groaning when she started rubbing in tight circles. I hummed my approval, leaning back to finish undoing my pants and releasing my hard cock from the confines of the fabric. "That's a good girl, use your fingers too."

She did, sliding two of her delicate fingers into her hungry cunt and finger-fucking herself while she rubbed her clit. The scent of her arousal surrounded me, and I'd let her get close to the edge, but not get quite there. That pleasure was reserved for me, and only I could bring her there.

Stroking my cock while watching her play with herself was the ultimate test to my willpower. But this was about torturing her and reminding her she was mine to own. Her orgasm approached quickly, and I didn't move fast enough.

"No!" I roared, grabbing her hand and wrenching it away from her pussy. But she was past the point of no return, and her eyes widened in fear before they squeezed shut with pleasure as her pussy twitched and throbbed. It may not have been as intense as the orgasms I gave her, but she still came, her body reacting on its own even without contact, and she whimpered as she came, her juices dripping onto my desk. When she opened her eyes, mine had darkened, and my fingers gripped her wrist. "Oh, you're in trouble now," I growled.

Cara squealed as I stood, grabbing her and yanking her to the edge of the desk. Something possessive flared inside me when I heard a giggle slip through as I slammed a palm onto her chest, pushing her back against the desk. Without bothering to undress further, I thrust my cock into her waiting cunt. Cara cried out, reaching up and grabbing at my tank top, but when I leaned forward over her, lifting one of her legs, I bit into her shoulder. Her cry of pain morphed into a satisfied moan, and the fabric of my top bunched up between her fingers.

"Oh fuck, Emrick!"

Thrusting into her harder, I pulled my lips from her neck and whispered in her ear, "Oh, I love to hear those dirty words from your mouth." She shuddered at my words, and I nipped at her ear. "But promise me you'll only talk like that to me."

"Yes, yes, I promise."

Reaching down and gripping her ass, I pounded into her pussy, forcing her to stretch around me. Sinking my teeth into her neck again, I groaned, tasting her delicious skin, sweet against my tongue. "I think I love you, pussycat," I mumbled.

Cara squealed again when I pushed into her deeper, wrapping her arms around my back. "What did you say?" she panted.

"I love you, and I don't care if you don't say it back. I want you, and I own you."

"Emrick, I—"

I filled her mouth with my tongue, not sure I wanted to hear what she was going to say. Evie had told me Cara loved me, but what if her *woman's intuition* was wrong. Zaqiel and his woman couldn't be trusted, not really. They both despised the business I was in, and I didn't blame them. They were both bright beings with light inside, and while I'm happy they found each other, I wasn't sure if I was ever destined for that sort of connection again.

But Cara, she was mine.

She had come back to me, and it was all the confirmation I needed.

Cara gasped when I pulled away from the kiss. Kissing her was so natural, and I made it rougher than it needed to be to hide the truth of how vulnerable it felt to kiss someone again.

"I love you too." She pushed the words out quickly, tumbling from those perfect lips of hers, perhaps afraid I was going to cut her off again. I smirked, groaning and closing my eyes for a moment to enjoy the feel of her around me as I thrust deep into her. Between moans, she said it again, a desperate whisper against my ear, "I love you too."

There were a lot of things unsaid, I understood that. She still would need time to understand and accept my true nature. There would be questions about Zaqiel and me, my brothers and sisters, God and demons, and Heaven and Hell. Those questions would come when the time was right, and the answers too. I wouldn't lie to her, but I would hold her so close she couldn't leave again.

There would even be a time when Tate would come back, and I felt invincible knowing she was with me. I would kill him. Maybe we could kill him together.

Time she could have to think, to do whatever. But I knew now, I couldn't live without her.

Without her, I'd go to a point of no return, and there would be nothing left to lose, including my soul.

Her legs trembled as she neared her peak, and I smiled against her neck as I reached between us, pinching and rubbing her clit and bringing her over the edge. I didn't stop when she came, pressing her past the wall of pleasure until she was squirming under my touch.

She'd come tonight over and over again until she was limp in my arms.

Then I would push her to that point one more time.

If she wasn't screaming my name, I wasn't doing it right.

Nipping at her shoulder and neck, I grabbed her hips again, tilting her up so I could drive in deeper.

"Come for me, Emrick," she panted.

I did, growling and grunting like the animal that lived within, emptying my seed into her, but I was far from done with her. She needed to be claimed several times for every day she was away from me.

She was in for a long night.

EPILOGUE

CARA

Emrick doesn't deal well with disobedience.

The truth still got to me sometimes, and I'd have to stop and take a moment to think about it. Emrick was an *angel,* or at least he used to be. Now he was one of the fallen. I'll admit that even after I came back to him, I still needed some time to go over it. Another few visits to Zaqiel and Evie, another few chats, and Zaqiel had even let me touch his wings and examine where they protruded from his back. They matched the scars on Emrick's back exactly, and my heart broke for him.

My love, he had only been trying to do what was right, what he thought was justice, and he had lost everything. I now understood the reason he took the path he did. He was so tainted now there was no going back to who he used to be.

But that didn't bother me because while we were probably bad influences on each other, neither of us cared.

Our love was dark and messed up, but it was still love.

Earlier today, I came back from one of my visits with Evie, needing to hear the same information again and again. She had told me her story, and I had confessed mine. We understood each other on a deeper level, even if we had dealt with our circumstances differently. I don't think we could ever be friends as such because she held a deep hatred for the business I was now a part of, but we understood each other, and that was something.

I hadn't told Emrick where I was going, and only when I came back had I confessed.

He didn't like I lied, or at least that I hadn't told him the full truth.

So, he needed to punish me.

In fact, I was being punished even as I walked the floor with a tray of drinks.

I still liked being part of the club, the thumping mess of a club that whirled around the business it hid and helped grow. While I didn't work full shifts and had the luxury of coming and going as I pleased, it also helped me keep an eye on the place, and the other bar and waitstaff were fountains of information. They heard and saw everything, and through me, that could be funneled to Emrick. We were on top of everything all the time, and our empire had strengthened in the past month.

The twinge of discomfort when I bent to place a tray on a table between a group of businessmen reminded me of my punishment—a sizable butt plug, which I was required to wear as I serviced the floor tonight. I knew Emrick would be watching from the balcony, his chin resting on the tips of his fingers and his eyes following me behind those dark sunglasses. He'd be smirking and just waiting for a hint I was going to break first.

But I wouldn't.

Or so I thought.

My legs buckled as I made my way back to the bar for the next order. Passersby grabbed my arms and helped me back onto my feet as I gripped onto a supporting beam.

"Are you okay?"

"Do I need to call someone?"

"Do you need some water?"

I waved them all away, a thin sheen of sweat on my forehead as I tried desperately to recover myself.

A vibrating butt plug—a detail he hadn't warned me about.

Nice touch.

I was surprised the remote activated from this

distance, or maybe he had been waiting until I got within range, serving a table that was closer to the balcony. Refusing to look up, I stood on shaking legs, the vibrations still pulsing through my body, and thanked those who had tried to help, swallowing past the moan that threatened to escape my lips.

With unsteady steps, I made my way up the stairs, meeting Sven at the top who was guarding the door.

"Emrick is calling me," I said, fully aware that my cheeks were flushed and certain the buzz of the plug was audible. His eyebrows shot up when I moaned as the vibrations increased in intensity, and I was forced to press a palm against the wall to keep myself steady.

Sven smirked. "Evidently."

"Let me through... *please*." I gritted my teeth, forcing my voice to remain steady when every nerve in my body was screaming at me to drop to my knees and rub my clit. Of course, by now, Sven knew who I was and my connection to Emrick.

I had no doubt he was acting on Emrick's orders to delay me.

My initial impression of Sven had been correct regarding the prison tattoos, but while I expected him to have done time for mass murder, judging by the look in his eye—although, who was I to judge—

it was aggravated assault that finally got him. They'd only found out about the money laundering, the fraud, and the murder after he was already incarcerated. He made a deal, and the DA wasn't happy to let him go with only eight years served. Who knows who he threw under the bus to save his ass. Sven was cunning but violent, and while we'd hardly be best friends, I wasn't afraid of him.

Provided I didn't get on his bad side.

Although, I almost smirked. I had Emrick's protection now. I was basically untouchable.

"Sven," I pushed the word out, grinding my teeth. "I'll get you back for this."

He chuckled, opening the door. "Sure you will, dollface."

Pushing past Sven, shoving him harder than necessary with my shoulder, I just about fell to my knees in front of Emrick as a smirk spread across his face. He hadn't lifted his chin from his hand, and while his dark glasses hid his eyes, I knew they'd be flashing with lust. Sven had mercifully closed the door behind me, but Emrick and I were s till visible to all the patrons and staff in the club. It took all my willpower to remain on my feet in front of him.

"If you bend over, I'll put you out of your misery," he practically purred.

"I'm not doing it here on the balcony," I hissed at him.

Chuckling as he stood, Emrick made his way to the door behind his seat. "Please…" he gestured, "…come into my office."

"Thank you." I stalked past him, holding my head high.

The moment the door was closed behind me, Emrick grabbed me, a rough touch that would have terrified anyone else. But I knew he wouldn't hurt me.

Not too far past my limits anyway.

He brought his lips close to mine and inhaled. Emrick always insisted if I were going to wear lip gloss that it be unscented. He didn't want to smell some artificial berry flavoring, he wanted to taste and smell only me. I thought he was going to kiss me and pursed my lips, waiting for contact that never came. He wrapped his arm around my waist and swept me across the office, forcing me to bend over the desk and holding me still as I squirmed. When he flipped up my skirt, I began rubbing my legs together, desperate for some friction against my clit.

"Shall I take it out for you, pussycat?" Emrick growled, tugging lightly on the plug.

"Yes, please," I begged. "Please, I can't take it anymore."

"Oh," he crooned. "I think you can."

Emrick began twirling the plug, and I moaned as it added to the sensation of the vibrations through my body. He was in complete control of my body, mind, and soul. Taking me as he needed and giving me what I desired. He touched a finger to my clit, adding only the slightest pressure. I was so worked up, it was almost enough to push me over the edge. But not yet. He wouldn't let me come, not after how I had upset him.

He unzipped his pants, and when I tried to turn to face him, he slapped my ass, then slammed a palm between my shoulder blades. He hadn't removed the plug yet, and the sensations were overwhelming me. When he began rubbing his cock against my pussy, I moaned, and he leaned forward, whispering in my ear, "Are you ready for your punishment, pussycat?"

This wasn't already my punishment?

"I—"

He bit into my shoulder, probably drawing blood, and I cried out. "That didn't sound like the right way to answer me." He growled. "I asked you if you're ready for your punishment?"

Another tug and twirl on the plug, and I moaned. "Yes, sir."

"Good." His voice was as dark as his eyes, and I trembled with anticipation of the impending pleasure and pain. I moaned again, knowing he was only making me wait to torture me.

He wanted it as bad as I did.

And I'd found the perfect match for my darkness.

The END

Next in the Unearthly Sins Series
Touch of a Demon

ACKNOWLEDGMENTS

I've used this section in previous books to thank those who have helped on the journey to becoming an author, and while I am and always will be grateful for their unconditional help and support, I think I need to take some time out to thank someone else.

You.

You, my reader, are so important to me. Because without you, these stories would be floating around with no one to enjoy them, and that feels inherently wrong. I can only hope that you love my characters and worlds as much as I do, that they bring you joy, and maybe after each book you get a book-hangover.

Not that I wish bad upon you, of course, but because

I want these worlds to capture you, to draw you in to the point where when you finish that last page and close the book, for a moment you're lost. *What do I do now?*

Because I've felt that way countless times, becoming so encapsulated within a story that when it's over, it's almost like grief, and I would love to bring my readers that experience and joy that can only come from fiction. Fantasy to escape reality. When we open those pages we *want* to be dragged into them, so, if only for a little while, we can forget whatever else is plaguing our minds and simply enjoy the story.

Random fact about me. A friend and I play a game sometimes in secondhand book stores, where we try to age a book simply by smelling the pages.
You'll react one of two ways to that—either think I'm strange, or you'll sit back, sigh, and think yes, there is nothing quite like the smell of books.

I got the age within three years once, that's my brag.

So, reader, I hope you loved this book, and I hope this and my other books and all the stories still to come make you happy.

Thank you x

ANGELS AND FIRE BOOKS
Find our exciting stories at:
www.angelsandfirebooks.com.au

READER GROUP

Want access to fun, prizes and sneak peeks?
Join my Facebook Reader Group.
https://www.facebook.com/groups/588038442170571

Stefanie Dawn

NEWSLETTER

Sign up for my Newsletter.
https://www.subscribepage.com/angelsandfirebooks

BOOKBUB

https://www.bookbub.com/authors/stefanie-dawn

GOODREADS

Add my books to your TBR list
on my Goodreads profile.
https://www.goodreads.com/author/
show/21761217.Stefanie_Dawn

AMAZON

https://www.amazon.com/author/stefaniedawn

WEBSITE

http://www.angelsandfirebooks.com.au/

INSTAGRAM

https://www.instagram.com/angelsandfirebooks

EMAIL

info@angelsandfirebooks.com.au

FACEBOOK

https://www.facebook.com/stefaniedawnwriter

About THE AUTHOR

Stefanie Dawn has been a writer and creative soul all her life **and** strives to give her readers stories they can escape into as they become absorbed in the worlds created.

When she isn't writing, Stefanie might be painting, reading, or watching movies. She loves the process of producing films as another form of storytelling. There's also a good chance she'll be baking some delicious treats—pretending she won't later regret consuming them—or simply enjoying a cocktail with friends.

Stefanie Dawn lives in South Australia with her ever-supportive partner and a lovable gang of rescue cats.

Stefanie Dawn

You can stay up to date with
Stefanie and her books at:
www.angelsandfirebooks.com.au

www.ingramcontent.com/pod-product-compliance
Lightning Source LLC
Chambersburg PA
CBHW051131190726
48290CB00006B/1787